"We've been set up..."

More shots were fired as Arielle hit the ground. She sought cover toward the back end of the sheriff's vehicle, pressing her back against the metal.

Neil reached in again for the radio to call for help.

More shots were fired.

He dropped the radio. "He's getting closer." He lifted his head just above the hood. Another shot ricocheted off the hood. "We need to make a run for it." He pointed toward the airplanes.

The shooter must be positioned closer to the front end of the car.

"You have your phone, don't you?"

"It's sitting on the console of the car. I'm not reaching in there again."

Arielle turned and lifted her head so she could look through the back seat windows. Though the image was distorted by two panes of glass and the dimming light, she could see a dark figure moving through the high grass by the forest and then settling into position.

The shooter was getting closer.

Neil was right. They weren't safe here...

Ever since she found the Nancy Drew books with the pink covers in her country school library, **Sharon Dunn** has loved mystery and suspense. Most of her books take place in Montana, where she lives with three nearly grown children and a hyper border collie. She lost her beloved husband of twenty-seven years to cancer in 2014. When she isn't writing, she loves to hike surrounded by God's beauty.

Books by Sharon Dunn

Love Inspired Suspense

Broken Trust
Zero Visibility
Montana Standoff
Top Secret Identity
Wilderness Target
Cold Case Justice
Mistaken Target
Fatal Vendetta
Big Sky Showdown
Hidden Away
In Too Deep
Wilderness Secrets
Mountain Captive
Undercover Threat
Alaskan Christmas Target
Undercover Mountain Pursuit
Crime Scene Cover-Up

Alaska K-9 Unit

Undercover Mission

Visit the Author Profile page at LoveInspired.com for more titles.

Crime Scene Cover-Up

Sharon Dunn

LOVE INSPIRED® SUSPENSE
INSPIRATIONAL ROMANCE

ISBN-13: 978-1-335-72315-4

Crime Scene Cover-Up

For questions and comments about the quality of this book, please contact us at CustomerService@Harlequin.com.

Love Inspired
22 Adelaide St. West, 41st Floor
Toronto, Ontario M5H 4E3, Canada
www.LoveInspired.com

Printed in U.S.A.

Though I walk in the midst of trouble, thou wilt
revive me: thou shalt stretch forth thine hand against the
wrath of mine enemies, and thy right hand shall save me.
—*Psalm* 138:7

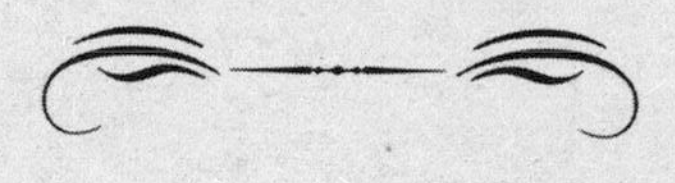

To all those who have walked the journey of loss and grief.

ONE

As she drove toward the crime scene not far from the small town of Silver Creek, Montana, FBI profiler Arielle Olson's stomach twisted into a knot. Why had the serial killer come back here to Wade County after more than two years? She checked her rearview mirror, not seeing anyone behind her on the road that led to the suburbs on the outskirts of town.

Being back here brought up a rush of unwelcome memories. The last time the bureau was in Silver Creek to investigate a murder, her husband, Craig, also an agent, had been killed in the line of duty. She'd found out she was pregnant with their daughter after his funeral.

Earlier in the day, she'd flown from her Denver office into an airport fifty miles from Silver Creek to investigate this second murder. After renting car and checking into the vacation home she'd reserved, she was prepared to see the crime scene. The rest of the team—two other agents—had arrived the day before. Not wanting to be away from her two-year-old daughter for any length of time, she had stayed later and arranged for her mother to drive up with Zoe. Her mother had texted her—they should be at the rental home before the day was over.

The man she was hunting had been named the Arson Killer because his trademark was to set the murder scene on fire.

Because most of the forensic evidence was literally burned up, the case relied heavily on her analysis as a profiler. She'd tracked this killer through four states, all in the west, and four other murders. Unless they were looking at a copycat, this would be the first time the killer had returned to the same area. Last time it had been a small town about twenty miles from this new crime scene, both in Wade County.

Her GPS vocalized directions. She'd been blessed to find a vacation rental in the country that was not too far from the county seat of Silver Creek. Arielle preferred to have quiet and privacy when she worked. The two other agents who had come up with her had gotten hotel rooms in town.

She'd agreed to meet Sheriff Cobain at the crime scene rather than ride with him in his car. The less time she spent with him, the better. Sheriff Neil Cobain had been on a stakeout with Craig the night he died. They were sitting outside a hotel room where they thought the killer was holed up. They had been given a misleading tip, and the man in the room was a violent meth dealer. From the time the sheriff had given her the news about Craig's death, she'd felt like he was not telling her the whole story. He wasn't a man who gave much away. If she had to venture an educated guess based on her ability to read nonverbal cues, she'd say he seemed to be holding back information. She wondered if there had been some poor decision making on the sheriff's part that had led to Craig's death.

The subdivision where the victim had been killed came into view. A crew-cab truck slipped in behind her and edged closer to her back bumper. She slowed down and drifted toward the shoulder of the road, thinking the truck wanted to pass. It remained behind her. She sped up, and the truck kept pace with her car.

Panic rising, she looked side to side. There was nothing out here but farmland. Her heart raced as she pressed the accelerator. The truck remained close.

Her phone rang. She touched the talk button.

The sheriff's warm baritone came across the line. "Everything okay? You're not having trouble finding the place, are you?"

Words seemed to stick in her throat. "I'm almost there… There's a truck behind me… I'm not sure what's going on."

Just then the truck sped up and tapped her bumper. Once, twice. The wheel jerked out of her hand, and she rolled down a small hill. Her car slid into a ditch and slammed against the bank. The impact hadn't been enough to make the airbags deploy.

Her whole body was shaking.

Her phone had slid across the console and landed on the floor. The sheriff's voice came on the line. "Agent Olson? Arielle?"

She uttered a sound but could not form cohesive words.

"Hang on. I'm on my way." The line went dead.

Her head cleared, and she was suddenly aware that the man who had run her off the road might be coming for her.

Her car had stopped at such an angle that when she went to push the car door open, it scraped on the ground and got stuck. She was trapped. She stretched her arm to grab her phone.

Trembling, she ran her hands through her hair and glanced around, not seeing any sign of the driver or truck. The rearview mirror provided only a partial view of the road. Her heart pounded when she saw truck tires. He was still up there.

She scooted across the seat and reached to see if she could open the passenger-side door. Her phone dinged. Thinking it might be Sheriff Cobain sending her a text, she pressed the message button.

Perhaps you'll die...next time.

Unable to focus, she stared through the windshield for a least five minutes. She gripped the phone, took a breath and checked the rearview mirror.

She had a view of legs moving toward her. Heart pounding, she braced for an attack.

When Neil Cobain peered into the driver's side window, he saw a very frightened Arielle Olson. He tried the door but was only able to pull it a few inches before it dragged in the mud.

"Hang on. Let me go around and get you out the other way."

Arielle rested her palm on her chest and gave him a quick, jerky nod. She held a phone with her other hand.

He ran around the car and yanked open the passenger-side door. She had already scooted partway across the seat.

Seeing her brought back a whirlwind of memories and unresolved emotions that he had to push aside.

He stuck his head inside the car. "Are you hurt? Can you move?"

"I don't think anything is broken." She swung her legs around to get out. planting her feet on the ground. When she moved to stand up, her knees buckled. He grabbed her around the waist.

"I've got you. You've had a terrible trauma here. What happened?"

"Someone ran me off the road." She shook her head in disbelief.

"Who ran you off the road?"

"A guy in a truck." She stared at her phone.

He saw the text message.

Perhaps you'll die...next time.

She drew the phone closer to her chest.

"Why don't you come up and sit in my patrol vehicle? We'll have to call a tow truck and have you checked out at the clinic."

She lifted her chin. "I'm fine physically. I came here to do a job."

He still supported her with his hand around her waist, and she did not pull away. "Just come and sit for a minute." The memory of her expression when he'd told her that Craig had been shot flashed through his mind. Such a hard loss. Something he understood. When he was twenty, his fiancée had died of cancer. Now at thirty-five, he had no intention of ever loving another woman and risking that kind of pain again.

She did not protest as he led her up the small hill and opened the passenger-side door of the patrol car. She still pressed the phone against her chest.

They were going to have to have a conversation about that text, but not while she was still in shock.

He left the passenger-side door open while he phoned Randy at the tow service in town and explained the situation.

He turned back to face Arielle. Her head rested against the back of the seat, and her eyes were closed.

She must have sensed he was looking in her direction, because she opened her eyes.

"Doing a little better?"

"I just needed to catch my breath." She sat up a little straighter. "I don't suppose you saw the truck?"

He shook his head. "I did see the back end of a truck as I approached."

"I was afraid he was going to—" Arielle's voice gave away her fear. "He must have seen you coming and been scared off."

"Do you remember what the truck looked like?"

She breathed in a staccato inhale. "A dark color, black or blue. A crew-cab truck with tinted windows."

Lot of people around here drove that kind of vehicle.

An awkward silence fell between them. It seemed like they should be able to say something about the events that had unfolded over two years ago, and yet the words had not come. He stepped away from the car and peered up the road, hoping to see the tow truck. Was the tension between them so intense that he couldn't even come up with some kind of small talk?

He paced up the road a few feet.

He was grateful when Randy's tow truck

rounded the curve. Randy parked his truck on the road and got out. He was a middle-aged man who covered his bald spot with a dirty baseball cap and had a bit of gut. The side of his truck said Randy's Garage.

Neil stepped forward and shook Randy's hand. "Thanks for coming so quickly."

Randy lifted the bill of his hat and scratched his forehead. "Rental car, huh?" He looked over at Arielle.

Neil was sure Randy recognized her. News of the fire and murder spread quickly in a county where the worst crime was the theft of a cow. "She was run off the road."

"Almost feels like big-city stuff, doesn't it? The fire and everything."

"You know we'll do everything to make sure we catch the guy this time."

Randy offered no response, only nodded. With Neil's help, he hooked up the car and pulled it out. Neil gave Randy a friendly slap on the back and a thank-you before Randy got in the tow truck and drove away.

He turned back to face Arielle. The color had come back into her cheeks. She pointed toward the tow truck. "I like how you're friends with everyone."

"It helps me do my job. People are more

likely to give up information and help out when they know they can trust you."

She crossed her arms and stared off to the side at some trees. "I know it is hard for the agents, as outsiders, to garner information." She turned to look at him, her gaze piercing with intent. "You were helpful in that way last time, and I assume you will be again."

There was much going unsaid in her remark. But it was the first time she had broached the previous investigation at all. She had laid out what her expectations were of him professionally.

"Both my deputy and I will be as much of a support as we can be."

"I'm ready to go examine the crime scene."

"I'll take you there." He stepped toward her. "But only if you agree to let Louise at the clinic check you out afterward. You were in a car crash, after all."

She shrugged and let out a heavy breath. "Okay, deal."

He got behind the wheel of the SUV and drove to what remained of the house. From the second he got in the car, he could feel the heaviness between them. He wanted to ask her about the threatening text and its connection to the accident. Silver Creek had never had any incidents of road rage like that. Arielle had just arrived hours ago. It didn't seem like someone would randomly run a stranger off the road. It must be connected to the case she'd come to investigate.

She stared through the windshield for a long moment. "I've read the prelim forensics report. As usual, there's not much evidence. It will be some time before they can even get an ID on the body."

"Your arson investigator was here this morning."

"I'm sure Agent Ferris will have his findings to me within a day."

"I had my deputy question all the neighbors as to what they saw in the days leading up to fire. Who they saw coming and going from the house, any strange cars that might have been parked outside the victim's house."

"Thanks. Have him send the report to me. Any information you can give me about the victim is helpful, too." Arielle's focus was on the blackened house in front of her. "As we gather more details, one of the agents might need to question the neighbors again."

Her remark felt like a barb. That she thought his deputy didn't know how to conduct an interview. He chose to let it go, knowing that so much of his reaction was about what had happened the last time she'd been in

Wade County. He'd really thought he would never see Arielle Olson again.

She pushed open the door of the car and stepped out.

He got out as well but stood beside the car. As he watched her circle the house and then step over where the entrance used to be, he glanced from side to side. A man who was probably the killer had just run her off the road less than a half mile away. Was he still close, waiting for another opportunity to harm Arielle?

TWO

As she walked the crime scene, Arielle found it hard to focus. A jumble of emotions rose to the surface. Someone had tried to run her off the road. The person in the truck probably would have killed her if the sheriff hadn't shown up. No one in this town knew her personally, but everyone probably knew who she and the other agents were and why they were here. In a small town faced with such a dark crime, news traveled fast. Had the person in the truck been the Arson Killer or just someone who didn't want them here? Maybe someone seeking to protect the killer.

As if that wasn't enough, being around Sheriff Cobain stirred her up, even though he had been nothing but professional. There was clearly something unresolved between them. Working with the sheriff and being back in the place where Craig had died brought up so much she thought she'd gotten past. From the moment she saw Neil it felt like she'd been run through a paper shredder.

She took in a cleansing breath and studied the charred house. Just as with the four other murders, she doubted there would be much evidence to work with. This case depended on what she could put together. The first step was to study the victims. So far there seemed to be very little they had in common. Two men and two women and now an older woman, different ages, different socioeconomic statuses, different parts of the west, but all rural and all lived alone. One of her tasks while she was here in Wade County was to rebuild the last days of the victim's life, to chart her movements, to find out whom she'd interacted with.

Sheriff Cobain stood behind her. "Sometimes it helps to talk things through."

She turned to face him. The wind ruffled his brown hair. All she saw in his wide brown eyes was kindness. If only he wasn't connected to her husband's death.

Maybe grief had skewed her ability to read the sheriff clearly. On a professional level, they had to work together if this case was to get any traction. She needed his help. "The normal avenues for building a profile seem to bring me up against a roadblock."

He stepped into the burned-out house. "You look at who the victims were, the crime scene and the organizational level of the crime, right?"

"Yes, exactly." His answer surprised her. She was flattered that he understood the details of her job.

He shrugged. "I took a class once."

Mentally, she chided herself for her own prejudice. She needed to quit making assumptions about him. "First, you look at the victims, to find some kind of pattern. But there's not a lot there. I have done countless interviews of people who knew each of the victims, retraced their steps days before the crime. Nothing stands out." She put her hands on her hips, still looking at the charred living room. "The crime scene yields very little because of the destruction of evidence."

"With the last murder, when you were here before, you said that the organizational level of the killer had to have been pretty high. Isn't that the third thing you look at?"

The words *when you were here before* echoed through her brain. For this kind of killer, breaking a pattern was significant. Before she'd been run off the road, she would have presumed that the killer had returned here because he had some kind of tie to the area. But now she wondered if she was part of the equation. What if he wanted to lure her back here, to a place of unresolved pain, to get rid of her?

A shiver ran down her back at the notion. She paced some more, taking in every detail of the house. "We know for sure he's highly conscientious. Nothing about his crimes seem to be impulsive. To find a time to set a house on fire when there will be no witnesses takes some calculation."

"In a county this sparsely populated, people notice when someone shows up or moves away. So that probably means he's in the community and part of it for some time before he commits the crime. If this is not a copycat, your theory last time was that he sticks around for a while so as not to draw attention by leaving right after the crime."

The possibility that this was a copycat had crossed her mind, too. "I think he has a pretty big ego. He likes to watch the aftermath of the damage he's done."

She looked around at the scorched living room—the blackened furniture, the half-burned curtains and everywhere the stench of smoke. From what she could see of what was left, the victim had had a taste for antiques. "Is there any way we can figure out the movements of the victim leading up to the day she died?"

"Her name was Betty Richards. No one had seen her for days. Betty had been talking about going to visit her son down in Atlanta. The neighbors thought she'd already left."

"Sorry. I shouldn't call her the victim. We get used to a certain dehumanizing vocabulary." She'd read the bare-bones profile of Betty Richards. Arielle looked around. The crime scene tape rippled in the wind. "Has the son been notified?"

"Yes. Betty was the kind of a woman who kept to herself. Lived here less than a year... The neighbors didn't seem to know a lot about her."

Her job was to try to get inside the mind of the person who had done this.

All the crime scenes were close to something that would attract tourists—a national park, a ski resort. One theory was that he was some sort of seasonal worker. It was helping to talk through the case. "Unless he is independently wealthy, which is a possibility, we are not sure how he finances his moves."

"Someone new to town would be noticed around here. Especially someone with money, unless they really kept it on the down low."

"Are you sure about that?"

He shifted his weight. “It’s possible a person could be holed up in a cabin somewhere out of town and fly under the radar.”

She examined each inch of the kitchen and living room. “We don’t know that much about the stats of our killer. We can conclude that the killer is probably a younger man, at least under forty, and probably in good shape based on the nature of the crimes and the physical strength required. The murders have occurred far enough apart that he would have time to establish himself in a community, so he wouldn’t call attention by being new, since he prefers small towns and rural areas.”

She walked the perimeter of what was left of the living room. The house was a single-level two bedroom. Even without seeing the arson report, it was clear the fire had been set in the living room. She suspected the manner in which it was started, the use of a timing device, would resemble the other crimes. She stared out a window that had been shattered, probably by the firefighters. Though the curtains were charred, it looked like they had been pulled shut to prevent the neighbors from seeing anything. This guy was methodical, not missing a single detail.

She clenched her teeth. In her time with the bureau, she’d closed a dozen important cases, but this one continued to elude her. She turned slowly, hoping something would pop out as significant. She'd already spent hours poring over the reports, witness statements and crime scene photos from all the previous crimes. But nothing compared to actually being at the crime scene.

"Do you need a minute alone? I can step outside."

Sheriff Cobain was being nothing but cooperative, and yet every time she looked at him, she thought of Craig. "Thank you." She appreciated that he seemed to understand her method for taking in a crime scene.

He left the house. She watched him walk past a side window where the curtain had been pulled open. He must be circling the perimeter, looking for any missed clues.

Arielle walked through the house to get a sense of who Betty was. The smoke damage made her throat feel gunked up, and she sneezed several times. The living room, where the body had been found, was nearly decimated. The fires might not be only to destroy evidence but part of the thrill of the process. Her investigation involved looking at other arson cases Agent Ferris dug up in each of the areas where the murders had occurred. Maybe the suspect had taken practice runs and left behind evidence.

She entered the victim's bedroom after peering in the other bedroom, which seemed to have been used as an office/craft and storage area. The bed was made. The room was tidy. By all appearances, Betty was an older woman of middle-class means. Arielle examined the contents of each of the bureau drawers. She opened and closed a jewelry box that contained only costume jewelry.

She finished walking through the house and met the sheriff outside.

"You ready to go?"

She nodded.

Once they were in the car and on the road, Sheriff Cobain spoke up. "After we go by the clinic to have you looked at, I can drop you off at the garage where your rental car was taken. Randy will probably have checked things out and at least know if he can get it running."

"Actually, I would rather be dropped off at the house where I'm staying. One of the other agents can give me a ride to the garage later." She wanted to get back to the vacation rental. Zoe and her mom should be there by now. "I really don't want to deal with a medical exam right now. I know I said I would, but I just can't. The clock is ticking on this case."

He tapped his thumbs on the steering wheel. "I can't make you do anything."

She was glad he didn't press the point.

They drove for several minutes in silence.

"So, what happened back there? It wasn't just a case of out-of-control road rage, was it? I saw the text."

She laced her fingers together and took in a breath even as her heart pounded. "Who else would be threatening me like that but the killer?"

"True, you haven't been her long enough for anyone to have a vendetta against you. So either it was the killer or you were chosen at random."

Arielle felt suddenly vulnerable. Not how she wanted to come across when she was around the sheriff. To work this case, she needed his help, but she also wanted to keep things professional. "It appears that way."

He entered the outskirts of town. Both stoplights were green as he rolled down Main Street. The town had a hardware store, two restaurants, a steak house and a Chinese place, and the usual collection of antique/thrift stores and a post office.

"Look, if you need some extra protection..."

"I'm sure the other agents will help me out." She hadn't intended for her comment to sound so defensive.

At the edge of town, they passed the sheriff's office, a brick building set apart from the rest of Main Street. "Suit yourself." His response was just a little curt. "I've got to be with you anyway as your tour guide for the county. I'm sure the other agents have their hands full. I just thought..."

This was so awkward. Maybe she could request the deputy help her out with interviews of locals and navigating the area.

She wasn't sure what to say.

They came to the edge of town. "Where are you staying?"

"It's the Stuben cabin."

"I heard they made that into a vacation rental."

He turned off on a two-lane road that wound past fields filled with cows.

"It has great Wi-Fi and is quiet, so I can work uninterrupted."

They pulled up to the cabin. Arielle saw her mother's car parked in the driveway. She got out in anticipation of seeing her daughter. The door burst open, and Zoe ran out with Denise Blake trailing behind the little girl.

"There's my ladybug." Arielle gathered

the love of her life into her arms, taking in the warmth and sweet toddler smell. Zoe's silky blond hair brushed against her cheek. She addressed her mother. "Did you have a good trip?"

"Zoe and I had a delightful drive," said Denise. "She was such a good girl."

Arielle swung around. Neil stood on the stone walkway. He had removed his cowboy hat and was twirling it around. Shock seemed to reverberate through his voice. "I didn't realize you had a child."

"Sheriff Cobain, this is Zoe, and my mom, Denise Blake."

Neil nodded. His lips pressed together, communicating uneasiness.

She put her daughter down on the ground. "Go on in with Grandy. Mama will be in in a second."

Zoe waved at the sheriff as Denise reached out for her tiny hand. Arielle waited until the door shut before turned to face the sheriff.

"She looks like her father." He seemed visibly shaken. "I didn't know."

"Neither did I. Not until days after the funeral."

"I am truly sorry about your husband." Neil's voice faltered.

"Me, too. It's been a tough couple of years.

Losing him and facing raising Zoe alone has made my faith deeper. That is strange gift of all this struggle. I couldn't do this single-mom thing without God." The tightness through her chest and throat indicated that talking about the past caused sadness she could normally keep in check to rise to the surface.

"It never should have happened…that night."

"What do you mean?" The level of accusation in her voice surprised her.

He opened his mouth as if to answer but then changed the subject. "Are you going to be okay out here…considering what happened on the road earlier?"

She didn't like that he was evasive. "I'll let the other agents know what happened. And, Sheriff Cobain, I know I spend most of my time hunched over a computer or reading reports, but I am a trained agent." Knowing that Zoe was going to be with her, she had locked her gun away.

"You might want to think about getting a place in town."

"I'll consider my options. Now, if you'll excuse me, I have work to do." She turned and headed toward the cabin. There was a part of her that wanted to revisit what he was about to say about Craig and a part of her that didn't want to know. It would only bring up more turmoil and make it harder to focus on her work.

She stepped inside the cabin, where Zoe waited for her on the sofa holding her favorite stuffed animal and a book. The house had an open layout without any walls between the kitchen and living room.

"Read me a story?"

Her mom was busy in the kitchen.

"Sure, honey." Work could wait. She'd read the files once Zoe went down for her nap or after bedtime. From the time she had found out she was pregnant, she'd vowed to make her little girl her priority.

Through the front window, she could see the sheriff get in his car and head down the long driveway. Did he have something to do with Craig's death? They had been the only two men on the stakeout that night.

"What on earth..." said Denise.

Arielle closed the book and angled her body toward the kitchen, where her mom was standing by the window. "What is it, Mom?"

"I think I saw someone in the backyard." The older woman stepped toward the window.

"Mom, stay back." Arielle bolted across the room just as she heard the sound of shattering glass.

Neil got to the end of the driveway and decided to take the long way into town. He needed time to think.

The night that Craig had made the impulsive choice that got him killed, Neil had later found an empty vodka bottle hidden in the back seat vehicle Craig had used for the stakeout. Neil had been watching from a different car. The alcohol had probably impaired Craig's judgment. To protect Arielle, to make sure that her last memory of her husband was a good one, he had not said anything. The official report had been vague on purpose.

Arielle's voice had been filled with suspicion when they'd begun to speak about the night of Craig's death. He didn't mind being thought of as the bad guy to protect her memory of her husband. And now he had that little girl to consider.

She was growing up without a dad. It was important that she believe her dead father had been an honorable man.

His phone rang.

Arielle's voice on the other end of the line sounded frantic. "Someone threw a brick through the window. I called you because I knew you'd still be close."

He did a giant U-turn on the dirt road. "I'm on my way. Did you see the guy or a vehicle?"

"He ran off into the woods. I think there is a road on the other side of the trees."

"I know which road that is. I'll send my deputy out that way to see if he can spot anything. I'm coming back to you."

"Zoe and my mom were so afraid. The brick almost hit my mom."

He pressed down on the accelerator. "I'll be there in just a couple of minutes. I need to hang up so I can radio my deputy."

"Okay. I've locked all the doors. Call me when you're outside. I'm going back into the bedroom with Zoe and my mom."

He heard a child cry out, fear permeating her sweet voice and piercing Neil's heart. Neil clicked his phone off. The idea of Zoe being afraid, let alone hurt by anyone, did not sit well with him.

Neil radioed his deputy, who was out on patrol not far from the road where the suspect had probably been. Neil would have checked the exit that led to the road himself if the deputy hadn't been so close. His priority needed to be getting back to the vacation rental.

He raced down the road that led to the little

house tucked away in the trees. He pressed the brake hard and reached for the door handle before he came to a full stop.

He sent Arielle a quick text.

Here, checking the perimeter of the house.

He circled the entire house, stopping at the broken kitchen window where the brick must have been thrown in. At this corner of the house, the trees were only a few feet away. He could see where the brush was broken and the grass trampled down. The road where the culprit could have parked was just a few hundred yards through the trees. This had to be the same guy who'd run her off the road. Solid police work meant he didn't jump to conclusions without evidence, but who else could it be besides the man Arielle had come up here to catch?

After checking to see that there was no one on the road, he headed back toward the house.

Arielle flung open the back door when he got close. She signaled for him to come in. Once inside, she spoke in a hushed tone.

"Mom is trying to put Zoe down for a nap. This was upsetting for both of them. I wanted to show you this while we're alone."

The brick rested on the counter. She picked up a piece of paper that sat beside it.

It was a typed note. *Always watching you. Waiting for my chance to kill you.*

"I grabbed the brick before Mom could see the note. My mother has enough on her plate trying to help me raise Zoe. She has a heart condition. I don't want to add stress to her life."

"We'll take the brick and the note in for evidence. He texted you in the previous incident. Maybe we can trace that phone."

"If this is our killer, it's probably a burner phone." She shook her head. "These kind of notes are meant to rattle me, just like the text."

"What are you saying?"

"This guy is like a cat with a mouse. He has to play with me before he kills me." Her hand fluttered to her neck, and she shuddered.

If psychological torment was this guy's MO, it was working. "It's not safe for you to be out here."

"I agree. The other agents can only be here sporadically anyway. They have a job to do as well."

"We need to find you a place in town," he said.

"I already called the hotels. They're all full. There's a fly-fishing tournament going on."

He rubbed his chin and stared at the shattered window. He just had one full-time deputy, Greg. To put him on protection duty would leave Neil seriously shorthanded.

"Why don't you come stay out at my parents' ranch house? My mom and dad are there, and we have a ranch hand who is around pretty much all the time. My house is just across the field."

Arielle's eyebrows drew closer together. He could tell she didn't like the idea.

Zoe stood at the edge of the kitchen. "You got horses?"

Mrs. Blake trailed behind her. "Sorry, she just did not want to go down for a nap."

Zoe held a stuffed animal that may have been a bunny at one time, though it looked well loved. She gazed up at Neil with wide brown eyes. Her blond waves framed her face.

"They do have horses and cows and pigs and chickens," Neil said.

Her eyes grew even wider as her mouth formed an O.

Whatever hesitation Arielle had, she seemed to be outvoted. "It's important that I have a quiet place to work."

"We can manage that," said Neil.

Mrs. Blake wandered over to the broken kitchen window. "Zoe, why don't you run and get your picture book about the farm to show this nice man?"

Zoe bounced away, disappearing into the bedroom.

Denise stepped toward her daughter. "Arielle, do you think the man that did this will come back? Probably just some teenager causing trouble, right?"

"Moving is just a precaution, Mom. We're kind of isolated out here." She looked at Neil. "It's just temporary until something in town opens up." Her words held a chilly quality.

"I'm sure it will be short term," Neil said.

Zoe returned, dragging her stuffed animal on the floor and holding a book with her other hand. "See." She held the book so Neil could grab it.

Neil took the book and flipped through it. "Oh, wow, lots of different kinds of animals."

Zoe drew the stuffed animal to her chest, popped her thumb in her mouth and swayed.

Mrs. Blake stepped forward. "Her favorites are the goats."

He stared at the simple pictures. And then down at Zoe, who focused her gaze on him. "We don't have goats. Do you like cats? We have some new baby kittens out in the barn."

Zoe nodded. "Babies."

Arielle stepped in. "We can get loaded up fairly quickly. We barely got unpacked. I have my files spread all over the office area. I will need to deal with those myself."

"I'll help you with the other stuff," Neil said. "Once you're loaded up, you can follow me out there."

"I'll get online and cancel the rest of our stay here." Mrs. Blake moved toward the kitchen, where there was a laptop sitting.

Arielle grabbed the threatening note before her mother could see it.

Neil handed the book back to Zoe. "Thank you for sharing your book with me."

Zoe gripped the book.

"What do you say, Zoe?"

She took thumb out of her mouth. "You're welcome."

Neil chuckled. "You can call me Neil."

"Zoe, come with Mama. We're going to put your clothes back in the suitcase."

With a backward glance at Neil, Zoe took her mother's hand.

Neil thought he heard the little girl say, "He's nice, Mama."

Mrs. Blake looked up from the computer. "Okay, our reservation here is canceled. I let them know about the broken window. This seems like a bit of an overreaction to me. That brick was probably just some kid doing a dare or something."

Neil chose his words carefully, keeping in mind that Arielle didn't want to cause the older woman any stress. "Could be. Why take a chance, though? What if it is a kid and he decides to come back and make more trouble?"

"Zoe is excited about your farm. That should be fun."

"Cute kid."

"It hasn't been easy. Fortunately, my daughter has an iron will and a deep faith."

Neil didn't know how much Mrs. Blake knew about Craig's death. Given that Arielle seemed to want to shield her mother and her daughter, she probably spoke of Craig's death in the vaguest of terms. "She does seem like a strong woman. Good at her job, for sure."

Mrs. Blake closed her laptop. "Her preference would be to be home with Zoe, at least while she is so young. But that is not how things worked out."

"I'm sorry about Craig," said Neil.

Mrs. Blake lifted her gaze as if she was looking at something far away in the distance. She simply shook her head and sighed. "She doesn't talk much about her work, but I know this is the county where Craig died. Strange. Don't know what God is up to with all this—Arielle's work bringing her back to a place of personal trauma."

"I'm not sure why history is repeating itself, either." Clearly, the killer wanted Arielle as vulnerable and unfocused as possible. Maybe that was why he'd come back to a place that would bring up so much personal pain for Arielle.

The older woman looked directly at Neil. "I guess we better get loaded up. I've only had a chance to open my suitcase and take out a few things."

"Once you're packed, bring your stuff out and I'll haul them to your car."

"Sounds good."

"I'll give my mom a call and let her know we're coming," Neil said.

"I hope we're not imposing," said Mrs. Blake.

Neil shrugged. "Not at all. Mom loves having guests. Any time a missionary family from church or anyone needs a place to stay, she's first in line to offer the guesthouse."

Within a half hour, everything was loaded into Denise's car, along with a few suitcases in the back of SUV. Arielle insisted on compiling her printed files herself as well as carrying her laptop.

Zoe still clung to her much-loved stuffed animal. “I want to ride with Mr. Neil.”

Arielle’s expression hardened, and she gave Neil a nervous glance. “We’re going in the car with Grandy.”

“Please, Mama.”

“Actually, Arielle, this car is stuffed to the gills with our suitcases and toys. It would make a little room if I could pull that car seat out. Why don’t you and Zoe both ride with the sheriff?”

Zoe bounced on her feet and watched her mother’s face.

“Okay.”

Something in her tone suggested she wasn’t overjoyed about the idea but couldn’t bear to disappoint her daughter.

“Great,” said Mrs. Blake. “I’ll grab Zoe’s car seat.”

Neil hoped the drive wouldn’t be too uncomfortable. Having Zoe around seemed to soften the tension between them.

He gave a final survey of the house while Arielle locked up. The words of the note echoed through his mind.

Always watching you. Waiting for my chance to kill you.

He had a job to do. He couldn't stay with them at the ranch around the clock. He prayed they'd be safe there.

THREE

While Zoe sat in the back seat and babbled about the different sounds farm animals made, Arielle glanced in the side and rear-view mirrors. Once they were on the main road, several cars had slipped in behind her mother's, but all had eventually turned off.

She caught Neil looking to see if they had been followed as well. His nervous glances and drumming his fingers on the steering wheel indicated he wasn't just checking to make sure her mom was able to stay close in her car. He was just as on edge as she was.

She had to assume that the threat the last note contained was going to be her new reality. The Arson Killer had lured her back here to kill her. Why did he think getting her out of the way was necessary? This was the longest stretch he'd gone without killing. Unless… Was there a case they hadn't yet connected to him where he'd gotten sloppy? She'd have to check with the bureau to find out what kind of open investigations they were looking at.

Arielle felt like she had been outvoted and dragged into going to the farm. But she didn't have a lot of options. She couldn't bear disappointing Zoe. Also, while she wasn't gung ho about having to spend even more time with Sheriff Cobain, it was clear that staying at the isolated vacation home would have been foolish.

She only hoped the quiet he'd promised her would be possible. The thought of being in a hotel meant she would have to deal with more noise and interruptions. What she needed right now was time to reread all the case files on the previous crimes while she waited for the reports from the new case to come in. There must be a pattern or similarity she was missing, some connection she needed to make.

Neil hit his blinker and slowed down.

The farm came into view—a house and several outbuildings surrounded by forest and mountains in the background. A corral, tractor and other farm equipment were visible behind the buildings as they got closer.

Arielle turned her head to talk to Zoe. "We're almost there, ladybug."

Zoe dropped her book on the seat, leaned

forward and then lifted her chin to try to see out the side window as she kicked her feet.

Arielle's heart leaped at the sight of her daughter's excitement. Sunshine seemed to follow this little girl around. Being with Zoe while she enjoyed the farm would take her mind off the case. The name Zoe meant *life*, and Arielle had chosen it for a reason. From the moment she'd first felt her daughter kick inside her womb, Arielle had felt alive again and filled with a sense of purpose despite the grief over losing Craig.

As they drew closer, she saw that there was a gravel road to the side of the big house, and a smaller structure was behind it. Neil drove directly up to the smaller building that looked like a workplace housing often seen on oil fields.

"This was once a bunkhouse, but the hired hands are usually local guys." He pulled up, and her mom parked beside him.

They both got out. As Arielle walked around the car to pull Zoe out of her car seat, he caught her, grasping her arm just above the elbow. "There's a room in there that would work as an office on the west end of the house. You can lock the door. I'm sure you don't want Zoe coming across the crime scene photos."

It warmed her heart to know that he was thinking of protecting Zoe. "Yes, thank you. That would be perfect."

She opened the door. Zoe fluttered her feet and wiggled in the chair. "I want to see da animals."

"Honey, we'll do that in just a little bit. Mom and Grandy need to unpack."

"I can take her," Neil said.

As kind as he was being, she wasn't about to turn her daughter over to someone who was still a stranger. "I'll take a few minutes and go with you." She reached in to unsnap the buckle and pull Zoe out of her car seat.

Zoe wrapped her arms around Arielle's neck and gave her a kiss on the cheek.

He glanced toward the house. "I'm sure my mom will be out in a minute to make introductions. Dad and the hand are out in the field somewhere. I should hang here until one of them comes back anyway."

"I'm sure we'll be okay if you need to get to work."

"Right now, unless I get called out, you are my work," he said.

The protective tone of his voice comforted her.

A tall woman with braided salt-and-pepper hair emerged from the back of the larger house and made her way toward them.

Denise had lifted the first suitcase out of the car and come to stand beside her daughter and granddaughter. “I can get started unpacking if you want to stroll around with Zoe.”

“I see kitty cats.” Zoe wiggled to be let down. She ran toward the nearby barn, where several cats had wandered out.

Feeling a sudden exhilaration, Arielle chased after her daughter, who bounced more than she ran. The little girl’s delight lifted Arielle’s spirits.

One of the cats, a calico, sauntered toward Zoe. Arielle knelt down. “I think she wants you to pet her.”

Behind her, she could hear her mother talking to the woman who must be Neil’s mom. The two women were already laughing.

Zoe reached out and touched the cat’s back. “So soft.”

Neil crouched beside her. “It’s a short walk to the pigpen and the barn where the horses are.”

“Yes, please,” said Zoe.

The three of them walked across the field. Zoe’s hand slipped into Neil’s. The little girl trusted so easily. Arielle reached for Zoe’s other hand.

They entered the barn, which smelled of hay and manure. Dust danced in circles in the sunlight streaming through the holes in the roof.

Zoe stopped, awestruck by the two horses as they ate in their stall.

"You want to pet one?"

Zoe nodded, still not able to close her mouth.

Neil gazed at Arielle. "If it's all right with Mom."

"Sure."

Neil gathered Zoe into his arms and walked over to the stall where a bay horse stood. "This is Rhonda. She likes people. Put your hand out."

The horse nickered and touched Zoe's open palm. Zoe laughed.

A bolt of pain shot through Arielle. It should have been Craig's job to introduce their daughter to these new experiences.

Arielle was about to step toward Neil and Zoe when her phone dinged that she had a text. Thinking it might be one of the other agents, she pulled it out. It was too dark to see the screen inside the barn, so she stepped toward the door.

Snuck away, did you? I will find you no matter what.

Her heartbeat thrumming in her ears seemed to grow louder, as though she had just put on headphones.

"Everything okay?"

Neil stepped toward her with Zoe in his arms.

"I'll tell you later." She stretched her arm out and touched her daughter's soft cheek. Zoe reached out for her, and Arielle gathered her daughter into her arms. She drew her close. "You're getting so big."

Zoe nuzzled against Arielle's neck. Being close to Zoe helped ease her fear.

Neil studied her for a long moment before changing his tone of voice to address Zoe. "Let's go look at the pigs. Mama pig just had some babies a bit ago."

The rest of the farm tour went by in a blur. She had a feeling she wouldn't be safe here for much longer. Somehow the text did not feel like an idle threat. It was clear the suspect had figured out they'd left the vacation rental but did not know where they'd gone.

Though she didn't like the idea of being away from her daughter or her mother, she wondered if it had been a mistake to have them come up here. So far, the threats had been directed at her, but the brick could have hit her mother, and it certainly had frightened Zoe.

The suspect could have hurt them or worse at the vacation home. Something must have scared him away after he threw the brick. Maybe he saw the sheriff's car as it pulled out. Once again, Neil's presence may have kept her safe.

As they toured around the pigpen and Zoe got to hold a baby piglet, Neil kept giving her nervous glances. He must have sensed that something bad was up.

Would Zoe and her mother be safer if she sent them back to Denver?

Neil lifted the squirming baby pig out of Zoe's hands. The little girl's excitement made him smile.

Zoe pressed her hands together. "Can't she stay wif me?"

Arielle knelt by her daughter. "Pigs are happiest when they are with their mama, honey."

Zoe crossed her arms and made a pouty face. "But I luv her."

The kid was so cute, Neil had a hard time keeping a straight face.

Arielle reached over and tucked a strand of wavy hair behind Zoe's ear. "We can come out to see the little piglets in just a bit. I need you to be a big girl now and go with Grandy. Can you do that for me?"

Zoe nodded.

"That's my girl." Arielle stood up and held her hand out toward Zoe.

Neil drew his attention back to where the two older women had been talking. "They must have gone inside. They looked to be becoming fast friends."

"Zoe, come on. Mama will take you inside, and then Mr. Cobain and I need to talk." She looked at him with a piercing gaze.

From the moment she'd gotten the text, he knew something was up. They took Zoe into the big house, where the two older women were in the kitchen sipping iced tea and visiting.

Neil and Arielle stepped outside. Neil closed the door while they stood on the porch that faced the road. "Looks like your mom and my mom are getting along." Seeing the worried expression on her face, which she'd managed to conceal when she was with Zoe, made him move toward her. "Let me guess. You got another threatening text."

"He knows we left the cabin. It's just a matter of time before he figures out where we've gone. Once he sees that I'm not checked into one of the two hotels in town, he'll start looking elsewhere. How hard will it be to connect me to you and then your parents?"

"There is no totally safe place for you to be. I think we need to think in terms of as much protection as possible."

She shook her head. "I can't have Mom and Zoe in the middle of this. He seems to only be after me, to want to torment me. But I can't take a chance. I don't know what to do. Maybe I should send them back to Denver, but Mom just drove up here, and I don't think it is good for me to be away from Zoe for days at a time."

He hated to see her in this much turmoil. "Honestly, I think the ranch is the safest place. My house is just across the field, and I can arrange for my deputy to do a patrol through here. I can let Dad and the ranch hand know that you've received threats."

Arielle's phone rang. She stepped away and took the call, answering with a single word and then saying, "No, I'd really rather talk to him in person. How long is he willing to wait?" She listened for a moment. "Okay, I'll be out there as fast as I can."

She hung up and looked at Neil. "That was

Agent Ferris. The victim's son phoned into the sheriff's office, and the deputy contacted one of the agents. The son just flew in to try to deal with things connected to his mother's death. He's some hotshot business guy. He's got to leave fairly quickly, but he agreed to let me interview him."

"Where are you supposed to meet him?"

"I guess there is a private landing strip outside town? He must have his own plane. He's going to be taking off within the hour."

"I can drive you there."

"I'll just let Mom and Zoe know where I've gone. Give me a second." While she stepped into the house, Neil bounded down the porch to his car.

He was turned around and waiting for her when she came outside. She got into the passenger seat with a backward glance to the house. "I hope they'll be okay."

The sun was setting as they headed out to the landing strip.

They approached the landing strip, which was just a long dirt runway. Neil noted that there were three small-engine planes. Usually there wasn't more than one. The increased number was probably due to the fly-fishing tournament. There was only a small shack-like structure close by. The rows of hangars where people stored and repaired their planes were visible in the distance.

They both got out of the sheriff's vehicle at the same time. "Where did this guy say he'd be?"

"Let me call Agent Ferris. I didn't think to ask him what the plane looked like."

The hairs on the back of Neil's neck tingled. Though the parking lot was some distance from the landing strip, he couldn't see anyone in the cockpits of any of the airplanes. No one was wandering around, either.

A rifle shot reverberated through the air. The phone Arielle had been holding shattered into pieces.

FOUR

Arielle's hand vibrated with pain from the impact of her phone being shot out of it. Fragments of the phone flew through the air and landed on the hard-packed dirt. Like a curtain lowering over her body, the paralysis of shock set in.

Only Neil shaking her arm brought her back to reality. "We've been set up." He pulled her toward the car. They both bent at the waist and sprinted.

The shooter must be hidden in the trees not too far from the runway. Neil reached for the passenger-side door handle, flung the door open and crawled in, scooting over to the driver's seat. Arielle climbed in behind him as the pinging of rifle shots hitting metal pierced her eardrums.

Before she had even closed the door, Neil turned the key in the ignition and hit the accelerator. He zoomed ahead, doing a wide arc to get turned around.

Halfway through the turn, she heard a thunking noise, and then the car lurched and jerked. Neil gripped the wheel so tightly his hands turned white. "He shot the tires out." He reached for the radio just as the window shattered.

Fragments of glass sprayed all over Arielle as she crouched low in the seat. Her side of the car still faced the forest where the shooter was. The next shot went straight through the windshield. Arielle covered her face and eyes with her arms as more glass rained down on her.

"Get out." Neil tugged on her sleeve as he opened the driver's-side door and dropped to the ground by the SUV.

Still shaken, she crawled across the seat, staying low enough so her face was parallel with the steering wheel. In order not to raise up high enough to be a target, she had to exit the car by sticking one foot out and then squeezing past the steering wheel.

More shots were fired. In response, Arielle hit the ground. She sought cover toward the back end of the sheriff's vehicle, pressing her back against the metal.

Neil reached in again for the radio to call for help but was stopped by more gunfire.

He dropped the radio. "He's getting closer." Neil eased toward the hood and lifted his head just above it. Another shot ricocheted off the car "We need to make a run for it." He pointed toward the airplanes.

The shooter must be positioned closer to the front end of the car.

Was giving up the cover that the car provided the best option? "You have your phone, don't you?"

"It's sitting on the console of the car. I'm not reaching in there again."

She turned and lifted her head so she could look through the back windows. Though the image was distorted by two panes of glass and the dimming light, she could see a dark figure moving through the high grass by the forest and then settling into position.

The shooter was closing in. Neil was right. They weren't safe here.

He cupped her shoulder. "I'll go first. Once he has lined up a shot on me, you'll have time to make it to the cover of the first plane."

Much was revealed about who Neil was as a man in that he was willing to risk being shot so she could get closer to safety.

"Okay."

He burst out and sprinted toward the first airplane. At first, she heard the pounding of his footsteps. As she crouched low and gripped the bumper, she braced for the sound of gunfire. He was almost to the cover the plane would provide before a shot was fired. She winced and took off running.

She made it to the first airplane as Neil dashed to the second. She ducked behind the wheels and peered out. In the twilight she could detect no movement, but she had to assume the shooter was out there.

Using the wheels as cover, she worked her way toward where Neil waited for her behind the last airplane. Off in the distance, the rectangular white structure of the three buildings that served as hangars seemed to shine in the dusk.

Who was out there in the waning light? It had to be the Arson Killer making good on his threat.

Out of breath, she came to stand beside Neil. She still wondered why they hadn't been fired on again. Maybe the shooter had realized they might find help at the hangar and had fled, not wanting to risk being caught. They had a short distance to run out in the open to make it to where the airplanes were stored.

"Let's get over to the trees." Neil had already started to move in that direction.

Though it meant covering some extra distance, the trees would shield them from view until they were within yards of the hangars. They darted the short distance between the last airplane and the tree line. She braced for gunfire, but only the silence of early evening reached her ears. Neil ran ahead of her, staying near the edge of the forest.

As they drew closer to the hangars, she saw that the two rectangular buildings in front each had three large garage-type doors. The third building was between and behind the other two. Lampposts at either end of the structures provided some illumination. She didn't see any signs of anyone around. There were smaller doors by each of the airplane-size doors where a person could walk through. Her spirit sank. It looked like everything was locked up and not occupied. There were no windows to reveal if lights were on anywhere—on this side of the structure, anyway.

"What if no one is here?"

Neil glanced over his shoulder. "Let's check the other hangar."

She wondered if it would be safe to go back to the disabled car and radio for help.

When they walked between the first two hangars, she saw that there were windows on the side, but both were dark. There was a gravel road between the lines of buildings. They stepped out and moved toward the third hangar, which had five airplane-size doors.

A truck idled at the far end of the longer buildings. Her hopes of rescue were dashed when the headlights blared on and the car zoomed toward them.

Adrenaline coursed through Neil as he wrapped his arms around Arielle and all but lifted her out of the way as the roar of the engine and the bright lights enveloped them. She slammed against the metal of the longer building of hangars.

Still feeling protective, he shielded her by staying close and keeping his arms wrapped around her. "You all right?"

She nodded but didn't speak.

Already he could hear the truck tires squeal as it turned around and prepared to come at them once again. He wouldn't be able to get at them with the truck if they stayed close to the building. The shooter would have to get out and approach them. Neil's hand hovered over his gun. He was prepared for that.

The truck revved its engine. No doubt, this

was the same guy they'd encountered at the landing strip. There was nothing to stop him from taking aim with the rifle again. He and Arielle couldn't move away from the building without being in the line of fire.

Arielle focused on the truck. "We need to get out of here."

She was thinking the same thing he was. "Stay close to the wall."

They both kept their backs against the metal siding and hurried toward the end of the building. The truck rolled forward slowly, as if the driver was trying to decide what his best option was. Neil, who was closest to the truck, drew his gun.

Leaving the headlights on, the driver opened the truck door. Though it was hard to see in the dim light, he must be resting his rifle on the window rim, preparing to line up a shot.

They both turned and sprinted toward the side of the building for cover.

Just as they reached the corner, the last small door swung open, and light flooded out of the hangar. An older man stared at them. "I thought a heard a ruckus out here. What is going on, Sheriff Cobain?"

Reaching for Arielle's arm, Neil pulled her in front of him and guided her across the threshold. As he stepped inside, he glanced up at the truck that had tried to run them down. The driver had gotten back in and shut the door.

Neil closed the door and drew his attention to the man in the hangar. He knew him by sight but not by name. He was one of the men who flew in and stayed mostly at his hunting cabin tucked back in the hills. He had tired eyes and thinning steel-colored hair combed flat.

The man knew Neil, though, as he'd called Neil by name. "It's police business. We need to use your phone."

The man stared at the gun in Neil's hand. Neil holstered his weapon.

From the looks of the hangar, the older man had been doing some mechanical work. The plane engine was exposed, and tools were scattered across the concrete floor. The pilot studied Neil for a long moment. "What was all that noise about? I thought I heard a truck go by."

There was no need to tell this man the details of what was going on. All Neil had to do was allay his suspicions. "There's a situation here, but you're in no danger if you stay inside. If I could use your phone to call my deputy, that would be a help."

The older man hesitated before responding. "Oh, sure, no problem." With a quick glance at Arielle, the man wandered toward his work bench. He returned and handed the phone to Neil before looking at Arielle. "You're that investigator from out of town. I heard about that fire. So sad."

"Yes, the sheriff and I are working closely on the case," said Arielle.

Neil dialed Greg's number and stepped away from the other two people. Arielle made small talk with the older man, steering him away from questions about the investigation.

Greg picked up after a couple of rings. Neil explained the situation, telling his deputy he needed to arrange for the sheriff's vehicle with the flat tires to be towed and that he and Arielle would need a ride.

He hung up and handed the phone back to the pilot. Neil stepped toward the door and opened it. He looked one way and then the other. The truck was nowhere in sight.

That didn't mean he wasn't out there waiting, maybe by the road that led into town. The truck was not one that looked familiar to him, but a black crew cab was pretty common. It sounded exactly like the vehicle that had run Arielle off the road.

He'd forgotten to tell Greg to be on the lookout for the truck.

Neil stepped over to the other man. "Thanks for helping us out."

"No problem. Glad to do it."

"I don't know if we were ever introduced. I've seen you downtown from time to time," Neil said.

"I'm Elmore Christie. I mostly fly up on the weekends from Reno."

Neil held out his hand. He spoke with Elmore some more about fishing and other things he liked to do when he was in this part of Montana.

Neil saw the flash of headlights in the side wall window. He looked over at Arielle. "Stay inside. I'll check it out."

His hand hovered over his gun as he opened the door and stuck his head out. Greg waited for him in the other sheriff's car. Neil thanked Elmore again and gestured for Arielle to follow him.

Elmore waved and wandered back over to his plane, scratching his head as he stared at the engine.

Neil and Arielle glanced around as they stepped out into the dark and walked the short distance to where Greg had parked. He had a feeling Arielle's stalker would not give up so easily. It was just a matter of time before he came after her again, and anybody who got in the way was collateral damage.

"I can sit in the back," Arielle said.

Neil held the door open for Arielle and then climbed into the front passenger seat.

"We need to be on the lookout for a black crew-cab truck. Tonight and moving forward."

"Matches the description of the vehicle that ran Agent Olson off the road earlier today."

"Exactly." He glanced over his shoulder at Arielle, who looked pensive. "Everything okay?"

"I'm thinking I shouldn't go back to the farm." She craned her neck to look out the back window. "I don't want to lead him to my mom and Zoe. Far as we know, they are still safe there."

"There's no place to stay in town," Neil said.

"Is there an empty jail cell?"

Greg replied, "No arrests so far."

"No safer place for me to be, right?"

"I'm on duty through the night. But if I get a call out, you'll be alone," said Greg.

"Like I said, I don't think there is any safer place than the sheriff's office right now." She turned toward Neil. "If that is all right with you. We can come up with a new plan in the morning."

They entered the city limits and pulled up to the sheriff's office. Neil's personal vehicle occupied one of the parking spaces.

The town was pretty quiet this time of night. Except for the two bars, the steak house and a convenience store, everything was closed.

Neil got out and opened the door for Arielle. "Greg can show me around. You're probably tired and need to get home."

"Okay, if that's what you want." Neil wasn't sure why it hurt him that she didn't want to be with him for a few minutes more.

Greg still sat in the SUV talking on the radio. He popped open the door and lifted his head. "I just got a drunk and disorderly call on the radio. I've got to deal with it. Could you help get Arielle settled?"

Arielle's posture stiffened.

"I can do that." Now he knew why her coldness bothered him so much. They had just been through a harrowing experience together. It seemed like she would show a little more trust toward him.

Greg sped off down the street. Neil ushered Arielle toward the entrance of the sheriff's office. "Do you remember the layout from the last time you were here?"

"I never went back in the jail cell area."

He opened the door and stepped aside so she could go in first. The office consisted of two desks and two doors that led to interview rooms. The bathroom was at the end of the hallway. A closed door on the other side led to the three jail cells.

"I need to call my mom and hear Zoe's voice before she goes to bed. I'm just going to tell her we're working through the night. I don't want her to worry."

He pointed toward the phone on his desk. She sat down and lifted the phone. Neil retrieved the keys that would open the cells as well as the door that led to the cells.

Arielle's tone as she talked to her mother and Zoe sounded strained, even though she was trying to be cheerful. She turned her back to him while she spoke.

Wanting to respect her privacy, he slipped into the hallway that led to the cells. He pulled a blanket and a pillow for her out of the storage closet.

Arielle staying here was not going to work long term.

He waited until her voice fell silent before returning to the office area. Her back was still to him. He watched her reach up and swipe at her eyes. She must be crying.

It was clear being separated from her daughter was hard on her.

He cleared his throat. "Got it ready for you."

She whirled around and managed a plastic smile. He led her back to the cell. She settled on the bed.

"You're the one who understands the mind of a killer. Why is the guy after you like this?"

She stared out the high, small window in the cell then looked back at him. "All indications are that the guy is a sociopath and also very vain. His pride has been hurt that I am after him and getting closer. That's one theory. The other is that he is so deranged in his thinking that he believes if he gets rid of me, the investigation will go away."

"Guess it doesn't matter. The point is we need to catch him." Neil returned to the office, intending to stay there until Greg returned. No way was he going to leave Arielle alone given what had happened already. It was clear that she needed protection—and that she would not be safe until the man who wanted her dead was caught.

FIVE

Arielle had just drifted off when a strange noise caused her to wake with a start. Light flashed across the high window of the jail cell. It could just be a car going by, though she didn't hear the sound of an engine or tires rolling on pavement. Fear gripped her when she realized that this jail cell did not face the street.

She sat up. The noise had been a scratching or scraping. She waited as the pounding of her own heart surrounded her. Was she so on edge that the noise had been in her dreams and not real at all?

Neil had left the jail cell open, so there was no danger of the door locking. She stepped out into the hallway, intending to get a drink of water, catch her breath and calm down. When she stepped into the office area, only one lamp was turned on. She was surprised to see Neil asleep in his chair. His cowboy hat covered half his face. His arms were crossed over his chest, and he snored lightly.

Stepping softly, she made her way toward where she remembered the restroom being.

Neil jerked awake and lifted his hat. “Everything all right?”

“Sorry, I didn’t mean to wake you. I’m surprised you’re still here.”

“Greg went on another call. I just thought I’d hang out here until he got back.”

There was something sweet about him sacrificing his time over concern for her safety. He must have officially been off duty hours ago. “I was just going to get a drink of water.”

He rose and walked over to a water cooler she hadn’t noticed before. He brought her a cup of water, which she took. His hand brushed briefly over hers. “You seem a little… shaky.” He bent his head and leaned closer to see her in the dim light.

She clutched the cup and took a sip of the cool liquid. “I saw a light and thought I heard someone scratching at my window. The noise could have just been in my head. I was half-asleep.”

“Outside your jail cell?”

She nodded.

“I’ll check it out.” Before she could object,

Neil headed toward the door and stepped out into the darkness.

Alone in the room, she was aware of a clock ticking. No cars went by on the street, and except for a flashing neon sign for a pawnshop across the street, the area was covered in shadows. Light flashed by the front window. That was probably Neil walking around the entire station.

She sat down on a bench by the door. A moment later, there was a scratching sound at the window that looked out onto the street. She jumped up and raced to the window. It was almost too dark to tell, but it looked as though someone had just run across the street, but she couldn't be sure.

Thinking she might at least get a look at the guy, she opened the door and stepped outside. If he came at her, she would have time to get back inside. As her eyes would adjusted to the darkness, her heart pounded as the cool breeze touched her skin. She couldn't see any movement across the street.

She turned when she heard footsteps. Neil held the flashlight low so it didn't blind her. His distinctive silhouette with a cowboy hat was easy enough to discern.

"Nothing," Neil said.

She had to let it go because she wasn't sure

if she had even seen or heard anything. "It may have been in my imagination. Guess I'm just really on edge."

He stepped toward her, standing close enough that she could smell his woodsy cologne. "Understandable. Let's get you back inside."

Feeling safer knowing that Neil was in the next room, Arielle retreated back to her bed. She adjusted her pillow and pulled the covers up to her shoulders.

Hours later, the sun streaming through the high window of the jail cell woke her. Despite the inner turmoil, she'd slept surprisingly well when she'd gone back to sleep the second time. She planted her feet and took a breath before rising and heading up the hallway. The other two cells were still empty.

In the office, Greg sat at computer typing. He looked up and smiled when she came in. "Sleep all right?"

"Eventually."

"Neil made arrangements for some stuff to be brought over for you." He pointed across the room at a table, where a grocery bag sat.

A new phone sat beside the bag, which contained toothpaste, a toothbrush and facial wipes. "How thoughtful."

"Neil can be like that. Estelle from the drugstore dropped the stuff off."

Her coldness toward Neil was almost involuntary. Being close to him automatically reminded her of what she'd lost. And yet, as she got to know him better, all she had seen was a caring man who wanted to keep the people he was sworn to protect safe. "Please tell him thank you for me."

"You can tell him yourself. He comes on duty here in about half an hour. I've got to go home and get some shut-eye."

That meant Neil must have only gotten a few hours of sleep. "Is it just the two of you?"

"We got a couple of retired guys who work part-time when needed."

She looked down at the stuff he'd gotten for her. "This was really nice of him."

"Neil is a good guy. I think he kind of understands what you went through because he lost his fiancée fifteen years ago. They were just a few years out of high school."

"I had no idea." Arielle felt like the wind had been knocked out of her. She'd made so many assumptions about Neil that just weren't so. "He certainly doesn't wear his heart on his sleeve, does he?"

Greg shook his head. "I know he doesn't talk a lot about personal things. Certainly not about Megan dying of cancer, but he's way more complicated than he lets on."

She gripped the bag that contained the toiletries. "And considerate."

Greg rose to his feet. "We did have a little break with that truck that tried to run you down."

"Really," she said.

"Neil suggested I look for stolen vehicle reports in neighboring counties. Sure enough, there was a black crew cab taken from Springdale County two days ago."

Her mind processed that information, trying to picture the movements of the man who had tried to take her life. "How far away is the place where the truck got stolen?"

"You could make it there and back in an hour and a half."

"I imagine sheriffs share crime reports."

"The more serious ones would have been on our radar."

So the killer had stolen a truck that wouldn't be quickly identified as stolen. "I'm going to go wash up."

"Sounds good. Neil should be in shortly," said Greg.

Arielle headed to the restroom, where she washed her face and neck with the cosmetic wipes and then brushed her teeth. When she returned to the main office, Greg was on his way out the door and Neil has situated himself at his desk. He offered her a soft smile when she entered the room.

"Got some hot coffee for you if you like."

She felt like she was seeing Neil for the first time. "Thanks for the phone and the other things."

"No problem." He focused his attention on his computer screen.

Greg said his goodbyes and left.

She walked over to the coffeepot and poured a cup for herself. "I was thinking that I could move my work to this office, if that's okay with you."

He took his hands off the keyboard and looked at her for a long moment. "Gonna be a lot of interruptions. Got people coming by all the time with issues."

"What do you suggest?"

"My house is just across the field from the farm. It would be quiet. Between the other agents and my help, we can check in with you to quite often as well as have a patrol go by there. We'll make sure you're not followed out there. Once I get off duty, I can walk with you across the field so you can be with your daughter and mom at night. The walk will keep you hidden from view for someone who is watching the roads."

She tensed but realized he'd probably presented her with the most viable solution. "If there is any indication that the killer has figured out where Mom and Zoe are, we will have to come up with a better plan. I can't risk their safety because of my job."

"I get that."

Neil clearly had put some thought into the plan and had realized how important it was to her to not be away from Zoe for too long and to have a quiet place to work. "I need my files and my laptop."

"I know you like to transport those yourself, but it would be best if I send one of my part-time deputies over to get them. We don't want to lead the killer to the farm."

"It does feel like he is watching me all the time. How did he know about Betty having a son in order to set us up at the airstrip?"

"It would have been easy enough to figure out. It's been in all the different local news outlets, and I'm sure everyone in town is talking as well. The message got to us indirectly from my deputy to one of the agents."

She sat down on the bench opposite of Neil's desk and took a sip of her coffee. The warm, dark liquid perked her up. "I need to stay in town and meet with the other agents. Agent Andrew Ferris is our arson expert. I'll talk to him at length. How the fire was set will verify that we are not dealing with a copycat. And maybe there will be some evidence to work with this time."

"Good, then I'll arrange for your files and laptop to be taken to my place. You can call your mom and let her know what is going on." Neil lowered his voice. "I know you want to protect your mom, but I think she needs to be given a few more details about the threat level you are under." He shrugged. "Just my two cents' worth of advice. What you do is up to you."

In the short time she'd been with Neil, so much had shifted for her. Yesterday, she would have interpreted his advice as wanting to control, but now she understood the deep compassion and concern behind what he said. "I think you're probably right."

"Dad, Mom and the hired hand will be on alert. I didn't give them any details, just enough to let them know to keep an eye on your mom and Zoe."

She took in a deep breath. "First things first, I need to talk to the other agents." She lifted the phone package. "And get this activated. Let them know my new number."

He returned to the desk, pulled scissors out of a drawer and handed them to her.

"If you like, I'll walk out with you once your phone is set up. The sheriff's vehicle was towed to Randy's Garage. I need to see if it's ready. You can check to see if your rental car is operational. I'm sure the rental company will cover the cost."

She thanked him. Once she had the phone working, they stepped out into the morning sunlight. It was about five blocks from the sheriff's cinder-block building to Randy's Garage, but the walk took almost twenty minutes because Neil stopped to say hello to almost everyone and ask them how they were doing.

As she watched him interact with senior citizens, dogs, children and strangers, she felt her heart softening toward him.

Neil had just finished patting a high school student on the back for his win at a track meet when she felt the press of a gaze on her back. She turned, studying the three-story building across the street. Plenty of people were milling around the shops, and the steak house had outdoor dining. It appeared they did a bustling breakfast business.

Several men gazed at her when she looked in their direction.

Neil cupped her shoulder. "Lot of strangers in town with that tournament."

A chill ran down her back as she remembered the words of the threatening text.

Always watching you.

As he worked through the day, Neil found himself distracted thinking about Arielle, worried for her safety. Certainly, she would be okay in town while she conferred with other agents.

Once they'd stopped by the garage, Randy had assured Arielle that her rental car should run fine. Neil had picked up the sheriff's vehicle with new tires and been sent out on a call ten miles outside town. Equipment had gone missing at an organic farm. Neil had talked to the foreman and gotten a description of the missing tractor, which he suspected would turn up in someone else's field or out on a low-traffic road. Teenagers had probably stolen it on a dare.

Now as he drove back toward town, he realized he had to perform his due diligence and check the places where used farm equipment was for sale just to make sure it hadn't been stolen and bought by one of the ranch supply stores. Though he could call one of his part-time deputies to escort Arielle out to his place and make sure she wasn't followed, he'd feel better if he was the one doing it. He hoped he wasn't out on a call when the message came through that she was ready to leave town.

Since meeting Zoe, he felt even more protective of Arielle. The little girl had already lost one parent. He smiled when he thought of the toddler's bright eyes and infectious smile.

As he drove down the long stretch of highway, a wave of sadness hit him. After fifteen years, thoughts of Megan and what might have been still reminded him of the chasm in his life. He'd tried dating other women five or so years after Megan had passed away. The experience only made him miss her more.

Until he had interacted with Zoe, he had viewed his life as very full. Work kept him busy. He helped coach baseball in the spring, and he had nieces and nephews he liked spending time with when he could get away for a visit. Had he missed out on something deeper by choosing not to marry and have children?

Neil hit his turn signal when the sign for the ranch supply place on the outskirts of town came into view.

Inside the store, Neil spoke to the manager,

who said he didn't think they'd gotten a tractor that matched the description of the stolen one, but he was welcome to walk the yard to double-check.

Neil stepped outside into the June sunshine. After he had his part-time deputy get Arielle's files and laptop from the farm, Neil had sent him out to the airstrip to see if he could find any shell casings or other evidence from when they had been shot at. There was not much else he could do to track the man who had tried to kill them. Greg had mentioned that the black truck was stolen.

Neil was almost done walking the yard when a text came through from Arielle.

All done in town.

He said a prayer of thanks that he would be the one to take her out to his house.

Can you sit tight for ten minutes?

Sure. Waiting on the bench outside the hotel.

He put his phone away and continued walking the yard where the used farm equipment was on display.

Neil got into his sheriff's vehicle, prepared

to make the short drive into town. Out of habit, he checked his rearview mirror once he was on the road.

Given all that had happened, he felt a sense of urgency to get to Arielle as quickly as possible.

SIX

Feeling on edge, Arielle rose from the bench where she'd been sitting thinking she could enjoy the sun while she waited for Neil. She felt more exposed and vulnerable outside than she'd thought she would be. The sidewalk was bustling with people. Judging from the way they were dressed, many of the people must be here for the five-day fishing tournament.

She returned to the busy lobby and texted Neil where to find her. Knowing what she had been through, Agent Ferris had offered to sit with her. She wanted time to catch her breath and be alone to think, so she had turned him down. As expected, the arson report had shown the same MO as the previous murders. Ferris and the other agent would spend their remaining time here interviewing and combing the crime scene for any evidence. If anything was found, it would be sent to the Quantico lab for analysis.

She chose a seat that faced the door and dialed her mother's number. Though she'd decided to wait until the evening to tell Mom in person about the attacks, she needed to hear Denise's and Zoe's voices. Her mother picked up on the second ring.

She heard laughter in the background that must be Neil's mom.

"Hi, Mom."

"You have a new phone number."

"Yes, long story. Just calling to see how you and Zoe are doing."

"Zoe is having the time of her life. She's outside right now feeding the pigs with Mr. Cobain."

So she wouldn't be able to hear Zoe's voice. "I'm so glad she's having fun." Arielle fought off her disappointment.

"I'm delighted we came here with you, Arielle. That was a good call," Denise said.

"I will catch up with you later this evening. I'm working at Neil's place through the day."

"That's just across the field, isn't it? Maybe I can bring Zoe by."

Arielle quelled the panic that rose up. "No, it would be better if I worked alone, and then I will be back at the farm early evening. If you get a moment, though, when Zoe comes inside, I would love to talk to her."

"Sure, sure, honey." Denise paused for a moment, then took in an audible breath. "I'm sure you have something you want to tell me."

She hadn't fooled her mother. The older woman must have picked up on the strain in her voice. "Yes, but it needs to wait." Neil entered the lobby, glancing one way and then the other before spotting her. "Gotta go. I'll catch up with you later."

A smile graced his face when he saw her. "Ready to go?"

She nodded. "My car is parked in the hotel lot."

"I'm up the street. Why don't we meet in the sheriff's office parking lot? I'll give you the address to my place and then escort you there."

"Sounds good."

He turned to go and then pivoted. "On second thought, I'll walk you out to your car. We still need to meet at the sheriff's office. I have to check in with Greg anyway."

His reaction reminded her that she had to assume she wasn't safe even to walk across a parking lot. Neil remained close to her as they took the back exit from the hotel and stepped out onto the concrete.

"Over there." She pointed toward her rental car.

Once they were standing by it, Neil said, "Can you unlock it? I need to make sure it's safe for you to drive."

She hadn't thought of the possibility of a bomb or someone tampering with her car.

Neil checked the interior and then crawled underneath before giving her the okay to get in.

"See you in a few," he said. He watched while she got in the car and backed out of the space.

She appreciated his thoroughness. She turned out onto the street and headed the few blocks up to the sheriff's office. She parked beside an old battered truck that she hadn't seen before.

Since he'd waited until she pulled out of the lot, Neil probably would be few minutes behind her. She opened the door and stepped inside the office. An older man sat at the desk Greg had occupied. He must be one of the part-time deputies Greg had mentioned. Maybe Greg had gone out on call.

"Hi. I'm Special Agent Arielle Olson."

"Neil told me about you. I'm Charlie Hawkins. I used to be the sheriff before I retired five years ago."

"I'm just waiting for Neil now."

The older man pushed buttons on his keyboard and then rose to his feet. "Got a couple of things coming off the printer." He walked up the hallway where the restroom was out of view. The printer must be there.

The phone rang.

"You want to get that?"

The deputy was pretty casual. "Sure." She reached for the phone. "Sheriff's Office, Wade County."

Silence came across the line. But it was clear there was someone on the other end of the line breathing.

"Who is this?"

"Always watching," said the voice on the other end of the line.

All the breath left her lungs as she slammed the phone down. The deputy came around the corner holding a stack of papers.

Arielle felt like the room was spinning around her.

The door to the sheriff's office opened, and Neil stepped inside. He rushed over to her.

"Arielle?"

Her voice came out in a hoarse whisper as her heart pounded. "How could he know I was here to call the landline?"

"The killer called you?"

She nodded feeling lightheaded.

Neil guided her to the bench perpendicular to the desks. He sat down beside her.

She heard Charlie make a comment as if he was at the end of a long tunnel. “Everything all right?”

Neil responded, “Could we have a moment alone?”

The deputy said something about going across the street to grab a coffee.

Arielle shook her head and tried to calm the fear boiling over inside her. “How could he know that I would pick up that phone?”

“He called you again. Did he say anything?”

She shook her head. “It had to be him. He just wanted to remind me that he is *always watching*.” Her palm rested on her chest where her heart was still beating wildly.

Neil turned and stared out the big front windows. “He could have seen you pull in here. There are a hundred places he could have had a view of the sheriff’s office and seen your car headed this way. If you hadn’t been the one to pick up the phone, he might have just hung up.”

Neil’s presence had a calming effect on her. “He doesn’t have my new phone number. So now he has to find some other way to torment me.”

Lack of foresight on the killer's part to shoot her phone out of her hand at the landing strip meant he'd have to find other ways to threaten her.

"We can trace the call," Neil said.

"Every lead is worth pursuing. I'm sure he used a burner phone, but you might be able to pinpoint where the call was made from based on which satellite it pinged off of."

It was too much to consider. She needed to focus on her part of the investigation. "I'm ready to go out to your place and work the case I came here to solve. I want this guy behind bars. He's made this very personal by toying with me like this."

He gave her the address and directions. "I'll follow you in the sheriff's vehicle."

Still feeling a bit numb, she stepped outside with Neil right behind her. She glanced across the street at an apartment building, a pawnshop and the coffee shop where the deputy must have gone. The latter had two outdoor tables where anyone could see people moving around through the large windows of the sheriff's office.

There was a clear view of the sheriff's parking lot all the way up the street.

Neil rested his hand on the back of her shoulder. "You ready?"

"That call was less than five minutes ago. He might still have eyes on the sheriff's office. He'll know we left together."

Neil nodded. "Why don't you go across the street and get a coffee? I'll take off and wait for you on the edge of town by the Welcome to Silver Creek sign. There is a grove of trees close to there. I'll park behind those."

"Okay."

Neil glanced around again. "Charlie will be just inside the office if anything happens. He's coming back over here now. I'll phone him and tell him to keep watch through the big windows."

She nodded and headed across the street. She put in her order for a coffee and waited. When she looked out the coffee shop window, she could see Charlie keeping watch. Neil had already disappeared.

She crossed the street holding her coffee. She couldn't shake the feeling that she was being observed. Instead of heading straight to her car, she stepped inside the sheriff's office.

"Everything all right?" Charlie shifted his weight and pushed his baseball cap back on his head.

"I just thought there should be a little bit of a delay between Neil leaving and me taking off." It occurred to her that appearing vulnerable, like she was driving somewhere alone without protection, could draw the killer out.

She texted Neil to let him know why she was delayed. She took several sips of the coffee before saying goodbye to Charlie and heading out the door.

Her heart beat a little faster as she got into her car and pulled out of the parking lot.

She pressed the gas and headed up the road. The Welcome to Silver Creek sign flashed in her rearview mirror as she reached the city limits and sped up. She tensed up until she saw Neil's SUV slip in behind her.

Neil remained close behind her. She realized how shaken she was by all the threats and assaults. That was part of the psychological game the killer was playing. He was inside her head now. She was braced for the next attack, and even if it never happened, she remained in a hypervigilant state.

And it made it that much harder for her focus on the investigation. That must be part of the killer's plan.

Her GPS told her to turn in a hundred yards. Neil's directions had been to look for particular landmarks. Up ahead she saw the large round hay bales and the aging motor home he had referenced.

She hit her turn signal and drove up the

gravel road that led to Neil's house, praying that her afternoon would be productive and safe.

Neil took in a deep breath when they finally got close to his house. Though there had been no sign that they'd been followed, he couldn't discount the possibility that the killer would eventually figure out where Arielle was working. It was clear that staying in town made her just as big a target as being out here. There was no safe place for her.

The road curved, and his house came into view. He never grew tired of seeing the log cabin surrounded by evergreens. He'd bought the portion of land from his parents right after high school graduation.

He and Megan had planned on living here and raising a family.

He shook his head at the sadness that rose up. For most people, life didn't turn out the way they'd planned. Arielle and Zoe's certainly hadn't.

Arielle pulled into the driveway and waited in her car. After the last invasive threat, she was clearly exercising extreme caution.

He parked beside her and got out. He always left his door unlocked, and today was no exception. It had allowed the deputy who picked up Arielle's files and laptop to set the stuff inside. He now realized that he needed to change his habits for as long as Arielle was here working the case.

She rolled down the window and stuck her head out.

"Let me check the place out before you go inside," said Neil.

She nodded and sat behind the wheel. He heard the car door locks click into place. She wasn't taking even the smallest chance.

Neil unsnapped the strap that held his gun in the holster. He circled around the cabin and then cleared the rooms inside before coming out on the porch and giving Arielle the all clear.

She got out of her car and met him on the porch. He'd left the door slightly ajar. He pushed it open and stepped across the threshold.

She followed him, taking in her surroundings.

He suddenly saw his place through her eyes. Her files and laptop had been neatly piled on the entryway table. He hurried across the room to pick up a coat he had left on the sofa.

He picked up the books that were piled by

his reading chair that faced the backyard. "Sorry, it's a little messy in here."

"It looks cozy. I have never enjoyed going into a house that feels like you can't get comfortable because it's more like a museum than a home."

He appreciated the kindness of her comment. "I'll show you where you can set up your work space."

He led her down a hallway and opened the door to the bedroom he had turned into his office. The room had a desk with some papers piled on it and bookshelves that took up most of three walls. A large window looked out on the backyard, where the forest was only feet away.

Neil tensed. Would Arielle be too much a target with that window there? At this point every possibility needed to be considered. He took a step toward the window.

"I think it's best to leave the curtains open, so I can see if someone is out there. Don't you agree?" Arielle moved toward him as she rested her gaze on him.

She was probably one of those people who read body language with extreme accuracy. Still it stunned him that she seemed to know exactly what he was thinking.

"I wish there was a truly safe place for you."

"Honestly, after what happened at the sheriff's office, I think this is the best we can do, and it's certainly conducive to me getting work done."

Light from the window washed over her and brought out the blond in her light brown hair. She watched him with wide brown eyes. He was struck by how beautiful she looked in that moment.

"You're probably right. I made arrangements for my deputies to come by and check on you. Maybe I'll ramp that up a little. I might come by myself. I'll also check in with you via phone if things get busy for me."

"I should get my stuff set up. I work best when everything is laid out in front of me."

"It's lunchtime. Why don't I fix us both something?" His reluctance to leave wasn't just because he felt protective of her. He enjoyed her company.

She touched her stomach. "I could use some food."

While she hauled her files to the office, he returned to his kitchen, praying that he had something edible he could share with her.

Twenty minutes later, she entered the kitchen, where he had thrown together barbecue pork sandwiches that were left over from a few days ago and some baked beans his mother had brought over for him.

"This looks delicious."

Though there was a table on the back porch, he had decided against eating outside. He grabbed two cans of lemonade out of the refrigerator. He didn't own a dining room table, so they ate at the counter. He stood on one side while she sat on a stool.

Both of them ate without talking until their plates were nearly empty.

She put her fork down. "That hit the spot, Neil." Her expression held a certain intensity as she locked eyes with him. "Thank you for everything you have done for me…and for Zoe and my mom. I wouldn't be able to be close to them if it wasn't for you and your family offering such great hospitality."

His heart beat a little faster when she looked at him that way. "No problem. Zoe is a beautiful little girl. I'm so sorry she has to grow up without a dad."

A flicker of changing emotion seemed evident in the tightness of her jaw, but her tone of voice remained the same. "I'd like to believe that Craig would have been a good father. But the last year or so of our marriage, he had changed. His moods were so erratic."

He realized then that Arielle probably didn't know that Craig had had a drinking problem. It was possible to hide it from someone who didn't know the signs. Vodka was odorless, and someone who didn't know anything about alcoholism might miss the signs. "Was he under a lot of stress at work?"

"For the most part no, but he got caught in a firefight on a case in Texas that I think traumatized him. He wouldn't talk about it or get help. After that, it just seemed like he got angry at the drop of a hat. I assumed it was PTSD fallout. I don't know if it will ever make sense."

Neil chose his words carefully. Would it give her some sense of closure if she knew the truth? "I think he might have been self-medicating."

"What are you talking about?" She gripped the edge of the counter and leaned toward him, shaking her head.

He grabbed the empty dishes and took them to the sink. He turned to face her. "I'm just saying I think he might have had a problem with alcohol. It's possible to hide a drinking problem if a person doesn't know what to look for. I had an uncle who died from excessive drinking. We didn't see the signs until it was too late."

She didn't respond right away, just kept looking at him. Finally, she shifted her weight and then drew her attention to the view out the window as an edginess came into her voice. "I just can't believe that was what was going on. Craig wouldn't have hidden something like that from me."

He knew better than to push the issue. It was a lot for her to think about. "I need to get back to work. I'll check in with you in just a bit."

She whirled around. Her expression had become harder as her brows knitted together. "I'm trained to read people. To detect underlying motives and behaviors. It doesn't make any sense that I wouldn't understand what was going on with my own husband."

"It's a lot to process, I know. I didn't mean to drop a bomb on you."

"Craig and I were married for three years. You knew him for less than a week. I might ask you what happened that night on surveillance. Why didn't Craig have backup?" Her voice filled with accusation. And just like that, they were back at square one.

"I got there minutes after he decided to go in alone." She was pretty upset. He knew things could spiral out of control if they kept talking.

He wasn't about to tell her about the empty vodka bottle in the back of the surveillance vehicle. The news that he had been drinking on duty would hit her even harder. He had said enough. It was clear it had just destroyed any trust that had built up between them. "I didn't do this to upset you or hurt you. You said he had become erratic in his emotional responses. I just thought it might help you put some puzzle pieces in place."

"I think I would have known if he was drinking. I would have smelled it on his breath or found empty containers." Though she remained fairly calm, he detected a faltering in her words that suggested she was agitated.

He knew from experience that people with drinking problems were good at hiding things. He was afraid that saying anything at this point would be a bad idea. It had probably been a mistake to bring this up at all.

She studied him for a long moment, pressing her lips together and then staring at the ceiling. "You're right. It's a lot to process. I think I better just go do my work. Thank you for lunch and for a place to get my job done."

He nodded and picked up his cowboy hat from the counter. He knew he needed to give her some time alone to think about what he'd said. "Please lock all the doors after I go. My deputies have your new number. They will text you before they come by."

She had taken several steps in the direction of his office when he followed after her. He felt conflicted. Knowing the truth would give her an explanation about Craig's death that made sense. He felt like he had turned her world upside down. He didn't want to leave her in a bad place. His hand brushed the back of her arm. "You going to be okay?"

She turned to face him. Fire raged in her eyes. "Right now, I need to focus on my job."

"What I've said here will go no farther than this room. It's important that Zoe thinks well of her father." To press any more would only make things worse. "I'll see you in a bit." He turned and stepped out onto the front porch. He heard the dead bolt click.

Once he was in his SUV, he took in a sharp breath and gripped the steering wheel. Why had he dared to try to share what he knew? He'd wanted to clear up her confusion about Craig's behavior to give her some closure. But there was something deeper going on. During lunch he realized he was starting to have feelings for her. He knew if they were to grow closer, there couldn't be secrets.

He shifted into Reverse. What did it matter now? He'd clearly blown it and pushed her away by thinking he needed to come clean about what he knew. He prayed they would at least be able to work together.

He glanced at his house in his rearview mirror, hoping she would be safe at his house.

SEVEN

After calling her mom and hearing Zoe's voice, Arielle settled in to work. She reread each of the crime scene, arson and forensic reports and then the transcripts of interviews done by people who had come forward to offer information about the days leading up to when the victims were killed. They were just beginning to piece together Betty's movements on the days before her death.

Only a few friends had surfaced. Betty hadn't belonged to any clubs or other things that would have connected her to people who might have helpful information. Arielle really needed to talk to Betty's son, who along with grandchildren was listed in the obituary as her surviving relatives. And she would prefer to do it in person.

She had learned through one of the other agents that the son, Luke, lived in Atlanta but wouldn't be able to fly in until later on a commercial jet, not a private plane. The information about the son and where he was from had been in the newspaper, so that explained how her killer had been able to set them up.

She found herself distracted and stopping to stare out the window way more often than usual. Neil had dropped a bomb in her lap concerning Craig. Maybe it was just her pride and that was the source of her anger. No one wants to admit that they didn't really know the person they were married to.

She didn't want to believe that she hadn't realized what was going on. Both she and Craig worked really long hours at the bureau. In a way, they had been drifting apart even before the firefight in Texas. All her energy had been focused on work until Zoe was born. Now she knew what mattered most in the world. She'd cut her caseload dramatically after Zoe was born.

Arielle ran her fingers through her hair while contemplating what Neil had said. The news had stirred her up for sure and brought her grief back to the surface. The one bright spot in the conversation was that Neil clearly wanted to protect Zoe's understanding of who her father had been. There were so many good things she could tell Zoe about Craig when she got older and started to ask questions.

Maybe she had blamed Neil for Craig's death so she didn't have to face the truth. As she had gotten to know him better, everything about Neil indicated that he was a good police officer with a lot of integrity.

She stared at the trees in Neil's backyard. Her breath caught, and she stepped away from the window. Had she seen movement between the tree trunks or was it just a trick of the light?

She double-checked that the doors were locked, made sure her phone was close and then returned to the office to look out the window while standing off to one side. Two deer, a doe and her fawn, had come out to graze on Neil's grass. That must have been the movement she'd seen in the trees.

She returned to rereading the reports that had come in related to Betty's death until her eyes felt grainy from focusing on the computer screen. Her phone buzzed beside her.

One of the deputies was coming to check on her. He asked that she stand by the window so he could see that she was okay when he pulled into the driveway. A few minutes later, a car that didn't have the sheriff's insignia on it pulled into the driveway.

Her heart beat a little faster as she stepped back from the window. Charlie, the older man she'd met earlier at the sheriff's station, got out of the car in full uniform. She stepped back toward the window and waved. He nodded and tipped his hat before disappearing around the side of the house. She heard him checking the back door to see it was locked and then circling the house.

She worked through the day, calling the other agents and Quantico to see if any new forensic information had surfaced or additional witnesses had come forward with helpful information.

The deputy came by again later in the day, and Neil called to check on her as well. Though she sensed tension between them, she asked him how his day had gone, hoping to smooth things over. He'd gotten caught up with helping highway patrol deal with an accident on the interstate. She found herself enjoying talking to him. There was something calming about the warm quality of his baritone voice.

Neil ended the conversation by saying, "You must be getting hungry. Feel free to grab a snack with whatever you can find. I should be home within the half hour. I'll walk you across the field to be with your daughter."

"Thanks, Neil." She hung up the phone.

Arielle hadn't realized her stomach was growling until Neil had said something. She found some peanut butter and crackers. From the conversation she'd had with her mother, she suspected that Denise and Neil's mom, Mary Ellen, were planning a big dinner, so she didn't want to eat too much.

Just as she was finishing her snack, the landline phone rang. She hurried across the room, thinking that maybe Neil was calling to say he'd been delayed by another call. She lifted the receiver. "Hello."

Silence, but someone was clearly on the other end of the line.

Her heart beat a little faster.

"So cozy with the sheriff. I know where you are."

It was the second time she'd heard the killer's distinct voice.

Though she was shaking, Arielle managed to make her voice sound authoritative. "You know we're getting close to catching you. That is what this is all about, isn't it?" While she had him on the line, she had an opportunity to learn more about him. What he said and how he said it would reveal much about him.

She heard only background noise—voices

in conversation and then a bell ringing. The caller hung up, as the other voices seemed to be directed at him. Was he in some kind of shop?

Arielle gripped the phone for a long moment. She quelled her fear and rapid heartbeat with a deep breath. The killer had given her information about who he was. Not only the sound of his voice, but he seemed to have been making the call from some sort of business. The bell ringing was the kind that was put above a door to indicate that someone had entered a store.

No number came up on the caller ID. She punched in *69 on the phone on the outside chance that the stalker had made the call from the business phone. The call didn't go through. The guy was too smart for that. He was still working from burner phones.

She heard a car in the driveway. She stood off to the side and angled her head to look out. Neil has just opened the door of his personal vehicle, an older-model truck.

She rushed toward the door and twisted the dead bolt. Seeing him calmed her down even more. She made a deliberate choice not to bring up their earlier conversation. If he could forget about it, she would, too.

"Hey," he said. "I'm sure you are ready to go see that little girl of yours."

She nodded, anxious to tell him about the phone call. "He found me again, Neil."

"What?"

"He called your landline. He knows I'm here. I'm worried he'll make the connection to where Zoe and Mom are."

"Does he even know you have a child and that she's here with you?"

"He hasn't mentioned it." She shook her head, feeling the agitation return. "I don't know how much he knows. I don't know if Mom and Zoe are in danger."

Neil nodded, not answering right away. "All the other doors are still locked?"

"Yes. Let me run in and get my purse and then you can lock up." She hurried inside and grabbed her purse off the side table in the living room.

When she stepped out onto the porch, Neil was waiting for her holding his keys. He slipped the key in the dead bolt. He pointed toward the side of the house. "It's about a fifteen-minute walk. If our suspect is watching for us on the road, he won't know that we've gone to the farm if we walk. Time enough for us to talk and come up with a plan for dealing with this."

They walked side by side through the trees that opened up into a flat field. She still didn't see the farmhouse or any of the other buildings right away.

He cleared his throat. "The stolen truck the killer used was found today. We'll dust for fingerprints."

"So he knows we would be on the lookout for it. Maybe if another stolen vehicle comes up, that will be a lead."

This wasn't the direction she'd thought the conversation would go. Neil hadn't given any direct comment about the killer calling his landline. He must still be trying to wrap his mind around what it meant for her staying there.

They walked past a tractor in a field where little green plants poked out of the ground. The evening sun warmed her skin. "I can't just keep moving. I think that is what he wants, to disrupt and delay my work if he can't get to me to kill me. He'll find me no matter where I go. But I can't put Mom and Zoe at risk."

Again, Neil didn't respond right away. He increased his pace, and she had to walk faster to keep up. Maybe his legs were moving at the rate of his thoughts. She wasn't sure what was going on with him.

* * *

Neil slowed down when the back side of the farm came into view. For the second time today, he felt like he had to have a hard conversation with Arielle. "You're going to talk to your mom about the level of danger you're in?"

"Yes, I was hoping to find some time alone with her tonight. I think she has kind of figured it out."

"That conversation needs to happen sooner rather than later." His worry over everyone's safety made his voice sound more forceful than he had intended.

"I agree," she said. "I'm just struggling with how to tell her in a way that adds the least amount of worry and stress. I know that shielding her at this point is not a good idea."

"I think you are right. We need to get your mom and Zoe to a different location. I know they don't appear to be the killer's target, but we need to be cautious."

She lifted her face toward the setting sun. The only sound was their footsteps on the soft ground. "I don't know how much he knows about my personal life. We can't be too safe at this point."

"Whether he knows or not, he figured out where you were staying more than once. This is a small town. People talk. How long before he makes the connection to my folks' place?"

She kept walking. The anguish he saw on her face made him reach out for her arm. "Arielle, I know this is upsetting."

She turned to face him. Her eyes filled with tears. "It's not that I disagree with you. This…man…delights in tormenting me. What would torture me more than to know that the two people who matter the most to me were in danger? I don't want that to happen."

Without thinking he reached up and brushed his hand over her cheek. He hated seeing her in so much pain. "I know it is important for you to be with your daughter. Maybe we can find a place for them that is close enough for us to arrange meetings when you are not working."

She tilted her head toward him as a tear rolled down her cheek. "I just never thought this was going to be my life. Mom and Zoe depend on me financially. If Craig…" She shook her head. "I can't think about what might have been. This is my life." She wiped the tears away from her cheeks. "I have so much to be grateful for."

Neil felt like a hole had been punched in his heart. Arielle was a brave, competent woman, but even she had a breaking point. As they continued walking, he struggled with what to say. Words did not come easily to him. He'd always thought of himself as more of a man of action.

"For sure, we just need to get Mom and Zoe to a safe place. Maybe a hotel in one of the surrounding towns, and then I don't have to send them back to Denver. I can't bear the thought of being separated from my daughter for days on end."

Neil nodded. "Not sure what to do. We need to make this happen tonight. I'm going to call some people to try to set something up."

They were within yards of one of the barns. As they drew closer, he heard the laughter a child and several adults.

Arielle took off running. He caught up with her just in time to see Zoe, delighted, scream, "Mommy."

Arielle gathered her daughter into her arms.

Neil took in the scene of his mom and dad holding hands standing close to the porch and Arielle's mother holding a wand that made bubbles. A few bubbles still floated in the air. Arielle drew her daughter even closer. "I missed you, ladybug."

"I missed you, too, Mommy."

In that moment, he vowed he would do

everything he could to ensure that Zoe, Denise and Arielle were kept safe. They needed to come up with a plan fast.

EIGHT

Arielle found herself not wanting to let go of Zoe. "Did you have a good day, ladybug?"

Zoe wrapped her arms around Arielle's neck. "I love it here, Mama."

She pulled back so she could bop Zoe on the nose.

Zoe nodded. "I fed animals and rode on Mr. Grandpa's tractor."

Her eyes searched her daughter's. "That sounds like fun."

Zoe pressed her hand on Arielle's cheek. "Are you sad, Mommy?"

"No, just thinking about some things, baby."

Denise rested her hand on Arielle's shoulder. "We've got fried chicken for dinner." Denise turned toward Neil's mom. "And Mary Ellen made some apple crisp for dessert."

"I helped," said Zoe.

Arielle rose to her feet and reached down to

pick up Zoe. "That sounds delicious, Mom." Eating dinner seemed like a time waster when danger was so close. But she had to balance that with keeping Zoe and her mom calm.

Her mother studied her a moment longer than was necessary. "Are you okay?"

"I've just got a lot on my mind, Mom." She glanced over at Neil. "Are you going to join us?"

"Sure," he said.

Something about the steadiness of his gaze helped calm her nerves, even though her mind felt like it was running a hundred miles an hour.

Neil's mom and dad continued to hold hands as they made their way up the porch.

Denise stepped in beside Arielle. "This has been so nice for both Zoe and me."

"I'm glad, Mom."

"It's not going to last, is it?"

Neil was behind them. "Do you want me to take Zoe inside so the two of you can talk?"

Arielle stroked her daughter's hair. "Are you okay with going with Mr. Neil?"

Zoe nodded. Neil reached out his arms for the little girl. As they walked away, he must have said something funny, because Zoe laughed.

Denise leaned toward Arielle. "Okay, spill it. I know that look on your face."

"I'll spare you to the gritty details, but bottom line, the man I'm trying to catch wants me out of the way."

Denise shook her head. "That brick that was thrown through the window wasn't just a random teenager, was it? What else has he tried to do to you?" The older woman's voice intensified.

"You don't need to know the details."

Denise's eyes glazed as she reached out for Arielle and drew her into a hug. "I have lost enough people in my life. I don't want to lose you."

Arielle hugged her mom back. She hated seeing her distressed. She pulled free. "It appears he is only targeting me, but we can't take any chances. Neil is working on finding a safe place for you to stay that is close by but not easy to find. That way, you don't have to go back to Denver, and I will still get to see the two of you, just not every night like we planned."

Denise stroked Arielle's hair. "This is a lot for you to deal with."

Arielle thought she might cry. "Don't know how I would do it without you, Mom."

"We'll get through this." Denise stepped

back so she could look her daughter in the eye. "You're a strong lady. There is a reason your name means 'lioness of God.'"

Right now, she didn't feel very strong. The relentlessness of the killer was wearing on her down, which might be his intent.

She heard footsteps on the porch. When she turned around, Neil was there.

"Mary Ellen and I worked very hard on this meal. Let's go enjoy it and we'll figure out what the next step is from there."

Neil waited for them as they made their way toward the porch. She noticed as they stepped inside that Neil took a quick survey of the whole area around the house before coming inside and closing the door. She offered him a nervous glance.

Arielle smelled the aromatic spices of the chicken and garlic mashed potatoes even before she sat down beside her daughter. Neil took a seat next to her.

Regardless of what lay ahead, she was determined to enjoy the meal and the company. Dishes were passed around and jokes were shared. She liked the way Neil's mom and dad still showed great affection for each other. Until her father had died five years ago, her parents had been the same way.

As much as she enjoyed the wonderful flavors and the company, Arielle's mind kept wandering. Zoe was struggling with her piece of chicken.

"Here, let me help you with that," Neil said and cut a piece off to make it easier for Zoe to eat.

He seemed to be a natural around kids.

Her cheeks felt hot, and her heart fluttered a little when he looked at her with that sort of half smile.

She was sure that his mind was probably distracted as well trying to come up with the best solution for keeping Zoe and her mom safe.

As soon as the meal was done and before dessert was served, Neil excused himself. While they ate the apple crisp and ice cream, she could hear him in the next room talking on his phone.

Her ears were half tuned into the conversation at the table and half listening to the one in the next room. She couldn't discern words but picked up on the intensity in Neil's voice.

Denise and Mary Ellen continued to talk about recipes and the best way to preserve produce from a garden while they cleaned up the kitchen. Ron Cobain moved into the living room. Zoe and Arielle followed him after the older women turned down her offer to help with the dishes.

Neil returned and sat down next to Arielle. "It's all set up," he whispered.

Neil's mom stood in the doorway between the living room and kitchen. "There's more apple crisp if you want some, Neil. I'd be glad to dish it up for you."

"No, thanks," Neil said.

Mary Ellen's hand brushed over Zoe's head as she headed toward the kitchen. Denise and Zoe seemed to fit right in with this family. Arielle didn't know if Neil had any siblings who had children.

The evening would have had a cozy feel to it if it wasn't for the threat that was foremost in her mind.

Neil invited Arielle out on the porch, where they could talk. Neil gripped the railing and watched the road by the house.

Arielle drew her jacket tighter around her shoulders to keep out the evening chill. "I've never asked you. Do you have brothers or sisters who have kids?"

"I have a sister with two boys and two girls, but she lives on the East Coast."

"I asked because your mom and dad seemed to have really taken to Zoe."

Neil stared at the porch. "That's the first

time you have ever asked me anything personal."

She had intended to keep things on the professional level at first, but so much had changed. "Guess I was curious." Her tone darkened. "It just seems when we get personal, things get kind of dark."

He shook his head. "You came here to do a job. I'm here to help you."

A wave of sadness swept over her. As ideal as the evening had seemed, they did better when they kept things professional.

The window was open, and she could hear Zoe talking to the family dog and an indoor cat while Ron joked with her.

Neil moved to the other side of the porch, away from the open window, and she followed. She could not put this off any longer. "So what is the plan?"

"I have a pastor friend in a town up the road about twenty miles. They have a guest room where Denise and Zoe can stay. The transport needs to happen tonight."

"It's already getting dark. I'm sure Mom doesn't want to be without her car. Are we going to escort her out there?"

"That way I can keep an eye on you, too. You shouldn't be alone."

"Both of us have put in a long day. I want

to spend as much time with Zoe as I can." Her voice faltered when she spoke about her daughter. "She's not going to be happy about leaving here."

He let out a small laugh. "She does seem to have taken to the place." Though fainter, she could still hear Zoe talking to the dog.

Arielle moved toward the edge of the porch. "I suppose we better go break the bad news to them." She gasped when she saw a flash of light by the barn closest to the house.

"What is it?"

"I thought I saw a light over there," said Arielle.

"Go inside and lock the doors. Get everyone to go into the den, where there are no windows."

As she hurried inside, Neil had already drawn his weapon and was headed down the stairs into the darkness.

Neil sprinted toward the barn where Arielle had pointed. He slowed down as he drew closer, tuning his ears to all the sounds around him. He could hear the horses inside the barn snorting and moving around in their stalls, clearly agitated.

He checked inside the barn, shining his flashlight up in the loft. He turned his flashlight off and stepped back outside and worked his way around the building. When he made it to the back side of the building, he thought he heard footsteps.

There was a flash of motion by the guesthouse. Then he heard what he thought were pounding footsteps. Neil took off running toward the sound. He circled around a large combine. Loose metal siding on one of the outbuildings creaked in the wind, making it hard to discern the sound of footsteps or any other noise. His eyes still hadn't fully adjusted to the darkness as he moved around the combine to face the field he and Arielle had walked across only hours before.

Again, he saw shadows moving in the field. He holstered but did not secure his weapon as he sprinted toward where he thought the culprit had gone. After running for only a few minutes, he slowed down when he came to cluster of trees and he could no longer see anything. Branches creaked in the wind. He moved to pull his flashlight out, suspecting that the suspect was hiding in the trees.

A force hit the back of his head with such intensity that his knees buckled. He struggled to stay on his feet as another blow with a hard object crashed against the middle of his back. He turned to face his attacker, swayed and fell to his knees. Little black dots filled his vision, and he feared he would lose consciousness.

As he fell on the ground, he heard someone calling his name. Arielle. But the voice sounded like she was very far away.

"Neil, are you okay?"

Though he was fighting to stay conscious, the fear that the attacker was close and would come after his prime target, Arielle, drove him to fight passing out. That might be why he was attacked in the first place, to lure Arielle out here. "You are not safe." The realization made him rally. He couldn't leave her out her alone and vulnerable.

Her arms wrapped around him. "Can you get up?"

"Did you see him?" His head throbbed with pain as he blinked over and over.

Still holding on to him, Arielle turned to stare out into the darkness. "I don't see anyone. Give me your gun...just in case."

He got to his feet and handed her the gun.

"He came after me with some kind of object."

"Let's get you back to the house," she said. "Can you walk okay? I need to be ready if he comes back."

Though the places where he'd been struck

still vibrated with pain, his head started to clear. "I think so."

Arielle glanced over her shoulder several times. The house came into view as they circled around the barn.

"What did you tell everyone?"

"I only told your dad what was going on. I didn't want to scare Zoe. Just that we thought there might be an intruder on the property and that they would be safer in the den."

"One more blow and I would have been out cold…or worse," said Neil.

Now that the killer knew Neil was Arielle's prime protector, it was clear he might try to get Neil out of the way to get to he or use him as bait.

"When it became clear your dad could protect everyone in the house, I realized it wasn't a good idea for you to be out there alone. I should have backed you up in the first place."

"You should have stayed in the house and sent my dad. It's you our suspect wants out of the way." They took the three steps up to the porch.

"You're probably right. I wasn't thinking. I was worried about you."

Neil reached out for the porch railing for support. "I think I'm going to be okay."

He pulled his phone out and texted his dad.

A moment later, they heard the locks slide open, and the senior Cobain eased the outside door open.

"All clear, Dad."

Ron opened the door even more and ushered them in. Neil knew that he needed to call a deputy to check on his house, which he was pretty sure was the direction the attacker had gone. He might have followed them across the field and been waiting for his chance. He hadn't realized that he and Arielle would be standing on the porch when she saw the light. They couldn't waste any more time—they needed to move Zoe and Denise.

"You all right, son?"

"He probably should be checked out by a doctor." Arielle walked beside Neil as they made their way inside.

He found himself reaching out for the wall for support. Arielle was right, but he had other priorities. "Let's focus on getting your mom and Zoe transported safely."

They entered the living room, where a rifle was propped against an easy chair. Dad must have pulled it out of the display case, intending to use it for self-defense.

"I'll go get the ladies," said Ron. He disappeared down a hallway.

Arielle stood beside Neil, touching his arm

lightly. "Are you sure you're okay? Maybe a deputy could escort us out to this place."

"Greg is the only one on duty, and I'm going to send him to watch my place to see if the guy shows up." He turned to face her. "I want to help you with this."

"Thank you, Neil. I appreciate it, and so do Zoe and my mom."

"The guy I'm taking them to stay with has some medical training. He can check me out."

When he saw the softening of her features as she gazed at him, he felt a connection to her that ran deeper than just wanting to do his job. Though he had tried more than once to date after losing Megan, it only brought up old grief. This was the first time he'd felt even a flicker of attraction. Too bad there was so much bad blood between them over what had happened before.

The women emerged from the hallway with Zoe in the lead, running toward her mother. Arielle gathered her in her arms. Denise and his mom entered the living room with Dad following behind.

Neil glanced out the window. Would the killer return?

Zoe ran her fingers through Arielle's hair. "Grandy says we have to go on another trip."

"Yes, baby."

Zoe nuzzled her face against Arielle's neck. "I like it here."

"I know you do."

"Will the kitties miss me?"

"I'm sure they will."

"I will miss them." Zoe sounded like she might start to cry.

He couldn't shake the sense of urgency he felt. It was clear that Zoe was confused by having to move again. He wanted her to feel at ease.

He knelt beside her and Arielle. "Tell you what. We'll make sure we take pictures of the kittens every day and send them to you. Would that be good?"

Zoe stuck her finger in her mouth as though she was considering the offer. "Can you make a movie of them playing?"

Mary Ellen stepped toward the little group. "I can send you two or three movies a day if you like."

"That would be good, huh?"

Zoe's expression brightened, and she nodded. "I will miss holding them."

"So sorry about this, sweetie." Arielle gathered Zoe into her arms and rose to her feet.

Denise stepped forward. "Is Neil going to lead us out there?"

"Yes, I'll get you the exact address as well so you can GPS it in case we get separated."

"Why don't you and Zoe ride with him? I need a little time to decompress and listen to my audiobook."

Denise looked and sounded tired. This was hard on everyone.

"Mom, I'm so sorry for all of this."

"I love you. We'll get through this together," Denise said. "Let's go get the car packed up."

"I'll give you a hand," Mary Ellen said.

Once the women had stepped outside, Neil looked at his dad. "Let me know if you see any sign of anyone on the property."

The older man pointed to the dog lying in the corner. "We'll walk the grounds before we go to bed." That would probably be enough to keep the killer away if he thought he could come back at them again.

Neil stepped outside. The illumination from the yard light revealed the women placing suitcases in Denise's car. Neil hurried down the stairs to give them a hand. Once they were loaded, he, Arielle and Zoe got into his sheriff's vehicle.

He did a slow turn around in the yard, allowing the headlight to illuminate the areas of the property that were in shadow.

When he drove toward the road, his mom and dad waved at him from the porch. Denise's car remained close behind as they got to the main road.

Minutes later, Arielle turned to check on Zoe in the back seat. "She's asleep already. Thank you for giving her the experience of being on the farm."

"Mom and Dad really seem to have taken to her. Wish she could have stayed longer."

"I know that this is a hassle, but it's late and I want to stay the night with Zoe. She has had enough shake-ups."

"We'll make that happen. As long as we're sure we're not followed." There was so little traffic at this hour, it would be easy enough to discern if the killer had followed them.

Assuming he had walked from Neil's place to the farm, he must have left his car some distance away. Neil theorized that the killer had followed them across the field or at least had seen which way they were walking.

As he drove through the darkness, he wondered if there was any safe place for this little family.

NINE

Arielle opened her eyes when sun shone through the window, warming her skin. Zoe was still asleep in her arms in the twin bed. Her mother, on the daybed on the opposite side of the room, had not stirred.

She heard voices in the kitchen and smelled bacon cooking. Pastor Eric Simon and his wife had welcomed them in last night. She estimated that they were in their late forties or early fifties. Judging from the brief conversation and the pictures on the wall, they had spent years as missionaries before coming back to Montana.

As carefully as she could, Arielle extricated her arm from underneath Zoe. The little girl stirred but did not wake up.

Arielle walked toward the sound of the voices and laughter into the kitchen. Not only was the smell of bacon heavy in the air, but the aroma of freshly brewed coffee drew her to the breakfast nook on the sunporch.

She was surprised to find Neil sitting with his friends.

"I assumed you had gone back to Silver Creek." Both of them had been so tired they hadn't really clarified what the plan was for today. She couldn't take her mom's car and leave her without transportation, so she had assumed she'd arrange for a ride from one of the other agents or a deputy.

Peggy Simon poured orange juice into a glass. "Neil insisted on staying in his car and keeping watch. I couldn't talk him into coming in and sleeping on the couch."

She met Neil's gaze. His eyes held deep warmth. "All in the line of duty, right?"

"You could say that." He pushed his chair back. "Unfortunately, I have to get going soon. I may have located a stolen tractor. If you want a ride, I can give you one."

Peggy held up two containers. "I've got breakfast all boxed up for you."

"And coffee to go," said Eric from the chair where he sat sipping his orange juice.

"Sure," said Arielle. "Let me just go kiss Zoe goodbye."

She hurried back down the hallway to the bedroom to touch Zoe's silky blond head and kiss her on the cheek. She watched her daughter sleep for a moment. The stuffed rabbit rested against her chest, and her hands curled inward.

Denise spoke from the bed across the room. Her eyes were open, but she hadn't yet sat up. "We'll be okay."

"I'll check in as soon as I can," Arielle said.

Her mom reached out a hand to her, and Arielle squeezed it before leaving the room.

Neil waited at the door, holding two containers. Eric placed the to-go cups in Arielle's hands.

"Here's to having a longer visit next time we see you," Eric said.

They hurried out into the sunshine and got into the sheriff's vehicle. Neil gave her the containers. While Neil backed the car out, Arielle took in a breath and glanced back at the house where her daughter would be staying. Nothing about this case had been easy.

"They will be safe here," said Neil.

"I know." She took a sip of the coffee, which was excellent—strong without being too bitter.

"I wanted to stay the night to make sure we hadn't been followed." Neil said. "Could you hand me my breakfast sandwich."

The car gained speed once he turned out on the street by the Simons' house.

Arielle opened the first container and handed Neil the breakfast sandwich. She took another sip of her coffee, not feeling like her stomach was ready for food just yet.

"Sorry you had to leave Zoe." Neil spoke between bites.

"This is better than her being all the way down in Denver. Years ago, when the profiler job was offered to me, I knew it was something that would be fulfilling and that I had an aptitude for. But I also took it because I knew it meant I wouldn't have to be in the field as much. I thought it would be safer. I thought it would be conducive to having children."

"I'm sure under normal circumstances it is." Neil left the city limits.

The SUV rolled down the highway. The traffic wasn't the caliber of what she experienced in Denver, but it was clear that people were out headed to work and other places.

"I got an interesting call from my deputy this morning. The ballistics came back on the bullets that were used in the rifle at the airstrip."

"What did you find out?"

"That the bullets were fired from an older-model 30.06 rifle, like something an antique dealer or collector might have."

She knew from experience not to dismiss any evidence out of hand. Sometimes the thing that looked insignificant ended up being the puzzle piece that brought the picture into focus. "Have him send me the full ballistic report."

"What is your plan for the day?"

"I don't want to move my office again," she said. "It will cost me too much valuable time, and I don't know that I'd be any safer."

Neil nodded. "I get that. Let me take care of this tractor issue, then I can stay with you. If I get another call, you'll just have to come with me. I can't leave you there alone now that he knows you're working from there."

That would cost her time, too. "What if we set up some cameras? You know, the simple ones that they use for home security. Catching him on tape would go a long way in identifying him."

Neil tapped the steering wheel. "I have some of those back at the sheriff's office. Easy enough to install."

"We can make him trying to come after me work to our advantage." A shiver ran down her spine. Her plan only worked as long as they got to the killer before he got to her. She was going to have to get out her gun, which she had securely packed away.

They passed several fields and a farmhouse set back from the road before coming to an area where several trucks sat. The vehicles, which were in various states of disrepair, clearly hadn't been driven in a long time and had been parked here to rust. A motor home with four flat tires looked like a more recent contribution to the graveyard.

Neil eased onto a shoulder of the road. He pulled the key out of the ignition. "You can come with me if you want. It's a nice day."

"What are we doing here, anyway?"

He pointed toward the motor home. "There was a report of a tractor on the other side of that thing. I'm going to see if it's the one that was reported stolen."

Arielle stepped out and crawled through the barbed-wire fence, which Neil held apart for her. Since turning off the highway, they had not seen a single person or car. Still, she was acutely aware that she was vulnerable at all times. In town or at Neil's isolated home, it didn't seem to matter.

She followed Neil around the motor home to where a tractor sat. Neil took a picture of it and pushed a few more buttons on his phone. "I sent the picture to the guy whose tractor was stolen. He'll let me know if it's his." Neil turned in half circle. "Figuring out who the thief is will take a little more doing."

"There was a farmhouse up the road," Arielle said.

"You just don't go around pointing fingers or even asking questions. That creates bad blood toward the sheriff's department. Something you never want in a sparsely populated county. First things first—if it is his tractor, he might just be happy getting it back. Honestly, the best thing to do is to let it go. People will start talking, and the thief will come forward."

She appreciated the patience Neil exercised in dealing with people and not ruffling feathers. "You seem to know how to do your job."

"Been at it for a while." He ambled back toward the truck. "Let's head in to the sheriff's office to pick up those cameras."

The drive to town took less than five minutes. When she got out of the SUV, Arielle glanced across the street at the three-story apartment building next to the pawnshop, the hardware store and coffee shop. The last time she was here, the killer had a view of the sheriff's building. Was it from across the street? Her gaze traveled the length of the building and the roof.

Neil looked up as well. "What are you thinking?"

"What if his ability to watch me is via a camera mounted somewhere?" She turned to face the street. "He could be in one of those apartments or inside the coffee shop—or miles from here watching a monitor."

"I can tell you the only camera on this building looks out on the street. We can view it from a monitor inside."

Neil ushered into the building. There was no one at the desks. She was fully aware that she might be watched even now. Because the windows were so large, it was hard to stand out of view of them without stepping in the hallway.

"I'll just be a minute." Neil disappeared into a back room.

She pressed he back against the wall and waited. She could hear cupboards opening and closing and then footsteps. She sat down in one of the office chairs and pushed it back into the shadows so she could see through the window but be out of sight.

She surveyed the early-morning activity on the street outside—people sitting at the bistro tables having coffee and a mom pushing a baby stroller.

Neil emerged holding four boxes. "Let's head out."

Arielle ate her breakfast sandwich while Neil drove back to his house. When he pulled into his driveway, he straightened his spine as he stared through the windshield at his front door. Something had alarmed him. He reached over and touched her shoulder. "Stay here. Lock the doors."

Her heartbeat drummed in her ears as she watched Neil pull out his gun and stalk toward the front door. Her heart pounded against her rib cage as she reached across to the driver's side of the SUV and clicked the button to lock all four doors.

Neil approached his house slowly, gripping the gun with both hands and remaining alert to his surroundings. His eye was trained to notice anything out of place. What had caused him to suspect someone had been there was that the wind chimes that hung on his porch lay on the ground. As if someone had pulled them down. Kind of weird, but maybe the sound had annoyed the killer.

There had been no strong winds last night. The loop for the chimes hung from a hook he had installed. Even if there had been a storm, he didn't think the chimes would have come down on their own. Also, the porch provided a degree of protection from harsh weather. The front door was secure. He ran his fingers over the keyhole where small, barely detectable scratches were present. Someone had tried to break in. Had they succeeded?

That's why they hadn't been followed. The killer had opted to come back here after attacking Neil on the farm. His deputy must have just missed him.

Neil pulled his keys out and opened the door. He cleared each room of the house and then entered the room Arielle was using as an office. The files were stacked neatly, and the laptop was closed. The files must have been what the killer was after or maybe he thought Arielle and Neil would come back here.

"It feels safer in the house than out there by myself." Arielle stood behind him.

He put his gun back in the holster. "It appears to be all clear."

Her expression changed as concern etched across her features. She took a step into the room. "He didn't make it inside?" Her voice came out in a hoarse whisper.

Neil did a quick survey of the room. "No. But there were signs he tried to break in."

She took a step toward her laptop. Her voice wavered, and she shook her head. "He could have destroyed my files. We have backup on everything, of course, but that would have set me back in a huge way. I'm tired of feeling like I'm in a war zone."

He rested his hand on her shoulder. She was shaking. He folded her into his arms and held her.

"I don't know how much more of this I can take."

While he held Arielle, his anger toward the killer smoldered. It tore at his heart to see her this upset.

After a few minutes, she pulled away and looked up at him. "The door was locked. You knew something was up even before you got out of the car. What tipped you off?"

"He took the wind chime down. Weird."

She stepped away and stared out the window that faced the backyard. "No, it's not weird, actually. It reveals something about his personality. The noise of the chimes was so distracting he had to pull them down. It suggests someone who needs quiet to focus. Plus, he didn't hang them back up. That means Mr. Meticulous is off his game." Arielle's hand trembled when she touched her cheek.

This was the most afraid he'd seen her since she'd been run off the road. He wrapped an arm around her back and squeezed her shoulder. She softened to his touch but was still clearly upset.

"We have to get this guy. I want this to be over." Her jaw grew hard as she lifted her chin. He appreciated the resolve he saw in her.

"Let me get those cameras set up," Neil said. "And I'll bag the wind chimes in case he left prints."

"I'm surprised he didn't set the place on fire in an attempt to destroy my work."

"Maybe he didn't have time. I sent my deputy over here to check things out last night after we left," Neil said. "I would like to get at least two other guys to be watching the house. He's going to come back. We would need to stop him before he ever gets inside or close to you."

"I can give you the other agents' numbers. They might be able to spare some hours. I think they are still combing the crime scene and trying to find any witnesses that might be able to fill in some blanks about Betty or anything they saw."

"I'll leave you alone to get some peace and quiet," Neil said. "I'll be close by in the house or just outside."

She flipped open her laptop and sat down

in the office chair. “Thank you. I hope I can focus enough to make some progress.”

He squeezed her shoulder. “I’m sure you will.” He stepped toward the door when her words stopped him in his tracks.

“I couldn’t do this without you, Neil. Thank you.”

He almost uttered that it was just him doing his job, but he knew that wasn’t true. This had become much more personal for him. He cared about Arielle and her daughter. “It has been my pleasure to help you out as much as I can.”

A sense of warmth and connection passed between them as she held him in her gaze. She turned away a moment later and drew her attention to the computer screen.

When he left the room, he could hear the start of a taped interview that she must have pulled up.

Once he was back in the living room, Neil grabbed the first camera, thinking about where it could not be readily seen and still pick up a useful visual. All the cameras would connect to an app on his phone. He decided to get a ladder and place one on the roof and another in a tree. That would provide a view of the driveway and the front yard as well as the front door. He removed his gun belt to make it easier to climb.

He pulled the ladder from the garage and got up on the roof to mount the camera. Once he was on the roof, he had a clear view of his property in all directions.

He could even see the roof of the most distant outbuilding at his parents' farm. A car parked on what used to be a road caught his attention. A man got out and jogged toward the trees that surrounded Neil's house. It looked like the man was carrying a rifle.

Adrenaline kicked into high gear as Neil crawled down the slanted roof back toward the ladder. He prayed he got to Arielle before the killer did.

He was almost to the bottom of the ladder when he heard the sound of shattering glass.

TEN

Glass sprayed across the office floor as Arielle plunged down to the carpet on her stomach.

"Arielle." Neil called her name from another room. She crawled toward the hallway as a second shot was fired.

She managed to squeak out a single word. "Here."

Once she was in the hallway, where there were no windows, she rose to her feet. Neil came down the hallway.

He stepped close to her, gripping her arm. "You okay?"

She nodded. "I'm not shot, if that's what you mean."

"Stay put. I called for backup. They should be here in a few minutes." His features hardened. "I took my gun belt off to mount the camera. I didn't have time to grab it."

Her gun was still packed away.

He sprinted toward the office, dropping to the ground when he crossed the threshold. There was more glass shattering in a different room. Neil darted back into the hallway.

"Where do you think that last shot came from?"

"I'm not sure. Maybe a window in the living room."

He gestured that she should stay put as he pressed his back against the wall. "I have a personal gun locked in a cabinet. Not sure if I can get to it without being a target. Need to figure out where he is. He seems to be circling the house." Neil made his way down the hallway toward the living room.

When he got to the end of the hallway, he stopped and looked back at her. Neil dropped to the ground and disappeared around the corner.

The silence was oppressive. What was going on? She couldn't even hear Neil moving around. Maybe he had taken up a covered position and was watching for the shooter.

She thought she heard sirens in the distance.

Her heart pounded as the seconds ticked by. She wanted to call out to Neil to see if he was okay. But that might give away where she was in the house.

A thumping sound came from somewhere in the house from the direction Neil had gone. The sirens drew closer. She thought she heard a rifle shot, but the high-pitched zing was hard to discern as the sirens grew louder. Backup must be close to the driveway.

She scrambled down the hallway on all fours to peer out into the living room. She took in a sharp breath when she saw Neil's legs and cowboy boots sticking out from behind an easy chair. He was lying on his back and not moving.

No. Please, God, no.

She crawled a few feet toward Neil.

The flashing lights of the sirens filled the window that faced the driveway.

She took in a stuttering, gasping breath as a hand went over her mouth and pulled her backward. As she struggled to break free and to cry out, strong arms dragged her away.

Cold metal pressed against her back. Where had the stalker gotten a handgun? It must be Neil's. She regretted not taking the time to dig hers out.

The lights on two police cars were still flashing.

"Looks like we have to go out the back way," the killer said.

His voice was gravelly and low. Just like the voice on the phone.

Still pressing his hand over her mouth so she couldn't scream, he pulled her down the hallway toward the back door.

There were two sheriff's cars out there. Did that mean only two men had shown up to help? Before she could see if that was the case, the killer had dragged her through the back door and outside. She had a limited view of the trees that surrounded the property.

The gun was still pressed in her back, and she feared if she tried to get away, he might just shoot her on the spot. She assumed that police procedure meant one man would seek entry to the house and the other would circle the outside.

What had happened to Neil? Was he okay?

The killer stopped in his tracks and let up the pressure of the gun on her back. What had caused him to freeze? She tried to glance to the side and caught a flash of motion in her peripheral vision. One of the officers must be coming this way.

The killer's grip on her had loosened. She moved to get away. He raised the gun to shoot her. He wore a mask over his face. The explosive power of the gunshot surrounded her, and then she was falling through space. As if she'd been thrown down a staircase, objects hit her back and head. She must have banged against the stairs and whatever else was by the back entrance.

She heard shouting. Someone running. The sounds were muffled, as though she had headphones on. The gunshot had caused partial hearing loss.

With some effort she raised her head. Everything seemed to be swirling around her. Her body screamed with pain, though she couldn't tell if she'd been shot or not. Still feeling like she might throw up, she reached out for the wall of the house.

She found her way to the back door. Using the wall for support, she made her way up the hall. She heard Greg, the deputy, talking into a radio in a panicked voice.

"He's lost a lot of blood. Get here fast."

Neil had been shot. The news made her want to double over in her pain. The back of her head throbbed, and she could not think straight.

Greg drew his attention to where she was standing. He pulled the radio away from his face. "What happened to you?"

She opened her mouth, but no words came out. Instead she touched the back of her head. When she looked at her hand, it was bloody.

Greg came toward her. "Whoa, you better sit down."

Arielle was pretty sure she hadn't been shot, just banged up by the fall. She found a seat. It took a moment for her to be able to speak, and even then, her voice sounded far away and frail. "Is Neil okay?"

Greg had dropped back down on the floor next to where Neil lay, not moving and probably unconscious. Neil's face was turned away from her.

Greg looked down at Neil, shaking his head.

The ambulance had arrived, and the EMTs entered the house.

Greg rose to his feet. "I think we've got two people here who need medical attention and transport."

Though she never totally lost consciousness, the medical treatment she received and the transport to the hospital went by in a blur. At some point the city policeman who had pursued the killer returned to say he had lost the guy but saw the car he drove off in.

She remembered being hooked up to an IV in the ambulance and seeing Neil, still not moving on a stretcher, on the other side of the ambulance. His shoulder was bloodstained. She longed to reach across the distance to squeeze his hand or stroke his hair, to let him know she was there and pulling for him.

But she could feel her own strength fading as the ambulance rolled down the country road.

Hours later, she woke up in the hospital in a dark room. She had no idea what time it was. Had her mother been notified about what had happened? She was wearing a hospital gown, which meant her personal stuff, including her phone, must have been stashed somewhere.

She stared at the ceiling as a realization sank in. There hadn't been time until now to process what had happened at Neil's house. She wasn't shot, but she was in rough shape and must have hit her head and back in an effort to get away. If the city cop had not come around the house when he did, she might be dead right now. The killer had clearly shot Neil to keep him from protecting her.

Taking in a deep breath, she sat up. When the room started to feel like it was spinning around her, she reached out for the rail of the hospital bed, gripping it until the dizziness subsided.

She pulled the cord to call a nurse.

Moments later, a nurse stuck her head in. "Good to see that you're awake. Do you feel up to eating? I could arrange for something to be sent up for you."

"What time is it?"

"It's about midnight."

"I've been asleep that long?" A whole day had been lost.

"Your body suffered a terrible trauma. It needed time to recover."

She touched the back of her head where it had been bandaged. "How is Sheriff Cobain? Did he… Is he—?"

"He's just down the hall. Still recovering from the surgery to remove the bullet from his shoulder. Fortunately, it didn't hit any vital organs."

Even if she could get her phone, it was too late at night to call her mother. "I could eat something maybe, but I think I'd like to get up and move around."

"The cafeteria is closed, but I can arrange for something to be brought to you. Are you sure you feel ready to get out of bed?"

"I have to get my strength back."

"Let me help you stand, and then you can decide if you would just like to sit in the room or maybe go down to the lounge at the end of the hall. Whatever you feel up to."

Arielle lifted the covers and swung her legs around. Even that small amount of physical activity zapped all her energy. She knew that the longer she didn't move around, the stiffer she would get.

"Take it slow," said the nurse. She angled her elbow so Arielle could use it for support. "When you're ready."

Her bare feet touched the cool floor. She was sore but managed a couple of steps with the nurse's help. After a few more steps, she was walking on her own. "I think I would like to stretch my legs. Is the lounge close?"

"Yes, just past the nurses' station. Not far at all. Are you comfortable to walk on your own?"

Arielle nodded. "I can hold on to the wall if I need to." It was important she get her strength back quickly. She needed to get back to work. Had the officers thought to lock up Neil's house?

"If you'd like, I can have a sandwich and drink brought to you."

Her stomach growled in response to the suggestion. "That would be great. Would you let me know when Sheriff Cobain wakes up?"

"Sure. He's just two doors down from you. This is a small hospital."

The nurse left. Once Arielle was in the hallway, she could see the lounge the nurse had referenced. The floor was completely empty.

Not even someone attending the nurses' station. There was probably minimal staff at this hour.

The first hospital room she walked past was empty. In the second one, she spotted Neil through the open door. Seeing his motionless body sent more shock waves through her. Though it was clear she would be okay physically, she had to admit that the attack had taken a toll her on her emotionally.

The lounge looked cozy and welcoming. She lowered herself into a plush chair that faced the window, where she could see the night sky and the twinkling stars.

A young man with a to-go container and a paper cup on a tray approached her. He was barely out of his teens, skinny and still battling acne.

"Are you Arielle?"

"Yes."

He set the tray on the table next to her chair. "Nurse Rachel thought hot tea might taste good. There is a sandwich in the container along with some sugar for your tea, if you like."

"Thank you."

She ate the sandwich and then sipped the tea while she stared out at the night sky.

Though she knew it was not a good time to

call her mother, her thoughts kept turning to Zoe. She finished her tea and stood up, perhaps too quickly. She found herself reaching for the nearest piece of furniture.

Arielle made her way back to her room, feeling a little more like she might be able to sleep. She walked past Neil's room. The door was open a sliver. A nurse must be in there taking his vitals.

She entered her room, where a bouquet of flowers sat on a table with wheels. A nurse stepped in behind her.

"Do you need some assistance getting back into bed?"

Arielle pointed at the flowers. "Did you see who brought those?"

"No, I was busy with a patient down the hall. They must have been brought in from outside. The gift shop is closed at this hour."

Feeling a rising sense of trepidation, she stepped toward the bouquet and pulled the card out.

It's all over for you. No one will keep you safe now.

Arielle whirled around. "He's in the building." She dropped the flowers on the floor.

"Who's in the building?"

"I need to get to the sheriff's room." She rushed toward the door.

Even before she stepped out into the hallway, she knew something was horribly wrong. Three people in medical uniforms rushed by, headed for Neil's room. One pushed a cart with medical equipment on it. She heard a loud beeping noise that must be a signal for some kind of emergency.

She swayed, feeling dizzy. The nurse caught her elbow.

"I think maybe you should sit down." The nurse guided her back in the room and helped her lower into a chair.

"Someone tried to kill Sheriff Cobain."

"What makes you say that? The emergency is probably connected to his gunshot wound."

This felt like an uphill battle, trying to explain everything that was going on. She didn't have the emotional or physical energy for this.

The nurse studied Arielle for a moment. "Why don't you sit and catch your breath?"

Arielle stared down at the flowers, where a few stray ones had fallen from the bouquet. "He's in the building. I need to find him."

The nurse still didn't sound convinced. "Who is in the building?"

She tried to stand but immediately sat back down. She was in no condition to do a search alone. "Please, I need my phone."

"You have sustained a blow to your head."

The nurse talked slower as if that would help Arielle understand.

"Please, just get my phone. It must be in my jacket pocket."

After walking across the room, the nurse opened a closet. She returned a moment later, handing Arielle her phone. Arielle blinked, trying to bring the keypad into focus.

"I think that maybe you should lie down."

Arielle shook her head. "That would leave me way too vulnerable. I can't be in this room alone. Help me get out to where there are people."

"The best thing for you is rest."

The nurse clearly wasn't understanding. "Please, I'm an FBI agent, and someone is trying to kill me. He's probably still in this building or has just left."

"Let me go talk to the doctor." It seemed the nurse was still running with the theory that the blow to Arielle's head was affecting her perception of reality. She hurried out of the room.

Arielle managed to press Agent Ferris's number.

Please, please wake up.

Agent Ferris's chipper, recorded voice came on the line. "I can't come to the phone right now, but leave a message and I'll get back to you as soon as I can."

"Andrew, I need your help. I need you to come to the hospital ASAP. The killer was here. He might still be."

Arielle turned sideways in the chair. She had no pocket for her phone. She braced one hand on the back of the chair and pushed herself up.

After making it out into the hallway, she rested her shoulder against the wall. A nurse with a very concerned look on her face hurried out of Neil's room and disappeared around the corner.

Still using the wall for support, Arielle took a few more steps down the hall. The frenzy of medical personnel shouting commands at each other from Neil's room almost made her collapse with fear.

Dear God, please, he has to make it.

ELEVEN

Before Arielle even made it partway down the hall, she knew she had overexerted herself. All that had happened was taking its toll on her mind and body. Another medical person exited Neil's room.

She wanted to know what had happened and if he was okay.

The nurse whom she had tried to convince earlier stood beside her. "Do you need some help getting back to your room?"

"Yes."

The nurse supported her by bracing her under her forearm.

"Have you heard what happened to Sheriff Cobain? Is he going to be okay?"

"If I did know, I couldn't disclose that without his permission."

They entered the room. The nurse guided her over to the bed. She sat down, and the nurse helped her lift her legs.

Arielle gripped the nurse's arm. "Please leave the door open. If you see anyone enter this room, come right away."

The nurse, who had a kind face, pulled the covers up to Arielle's chin. "The best thing for you is to get some rest."

"Promise me. You'll watch the room." Her voice held an intensity driven by fear.

"I'll do my best."

She handed the nurse the phone. "Can you set that close by so I can grab it if I need to?"

The nurse put the phone on the rolling tray and scooted the tray within arm's reach. She lifted the call button, wrapped the cord around the railing and set it beside Arielle's hand.

"I'm close. All you have to do is push that button."

"Thank you." Arielle's body was tired, but her mind was still racing. Her hand rested on top of the call button.

"I can bring you something to help you sleep."

"No, thank you." The last thing she needed was to be so out of it that she couldn't respond if the killer did come back.

The nurse picked up the flowers and set them on the windowsill, tossing the greenery that had fallen from the bouquet.

Arielle listened to the nurse's soft footfall as she retreated. The door was left open, and light from the hallway spilled in. She fought the exhaustion for as long as she could. This had all been too much.

She fell asleep hoping, praying that Neil was okay and that it wasn't sabotage that had caused the medical emergency.

She awoke hours later, still groggy. The room was dark and the hallway silent. She pulled herself into a sitting position and reached to check her phone. Agent Ferris had not texted or called. Of course not. Everyone was asleep. Her phone said it was three in the morning.

Arielle thought about seeing if the nurse could tell her if Neil was okay, but she found herself fading even as she gripped the call button. She fell back asleep.

Hours later, she awoke with a start. Someone was in her room. She jerked when a hand wrapped around her upper arm.

"It's all right. I just need to take your vitals." The gentle voice of the nurse seemed to be floating in the room. Arielle never fully woke up while the nurse checked on her.

When she did open her eyes for good, daylight streamed through the blinds on the window. She lifted her head. Agent Ferris sat in a chair at the end of the bed looking at his phone. His gray hair made him look older than forty-two.

"Hey, sleepyhead. Sorry I slept through your call."

The killer was probably long gone by now. "Like I said in the call, the suspect was here in the building last night."

Agent Ferris rose slightly from his seat. "Man. I'm sorry. I could have done a search. You don't look so good."

She waved his concern away with his hand. "He probably left right after dumping flowers with a threatening note in my room. If I hadn't chosen to eat in the lounge, he might have killed me while I was alone in my room."

"Kind of concerning that he was able to sneak in like that."

She pushed herself into a sitting position. "Sheriff Cobain had some kind of emergency last night. I'm scared that the killer might have tried to disable or even kill him since he has been protecting me. The suspect needs Neil out of the way. Please, could you find out what is going on with Sheriff Cobain. Is he okay?"

"I heard he sustained a gunshot wound. I should have come by sooner. Agent Davis and I spent the whole day combing through the ashes of the crime scene."

"Did you come up with anything?"

"No. I feel like we have checked all the boxes as to what the crime scene can tell us."

Even more reason why she needed to dig into the investigation. "You guys will be heading back to Denver soon?"

"I think we have collected all the evidence we can. There are some other cases I need to put my attention to—fires down in Arizona on federal land."

"I keep wondering what triggered this guy to kill again after thirty-three months. It's clear he came back to lure me here where I felt vulnerable."

"Are you thinking we might have missed a case that should have been linked to him?"

"Maybe, but something made him panic and break his pattern. Something triggered him to want to get rid of me."

"I'll pull up anything that might be important."

Other than talking to Betty's son, she would be able to return to Denver soon as well. "Can you find out what is going on with Sheriff Cobain?"

"I'm not family. The medical staff isn't going to tell me anything."

"You're a professional investigator," she said. "I'm sure you can get the information somehow."

An amused smile emerged. He rose to his feet and let out a theatrical sigh. "I'll see what I can find out." Agent Ferris left the room.

They'd worked together long enough on this serial killer case that they knew each other well enough to joke around.

Feeling much stronger, Arielle got out of bed. The rest had done her good. She found the bag that contained her clothes, stepped into the bathroom and got dressed. No way was she spending another day in this hospital. She needed a comb and a toothbrush.

Thinking that maybe the rooms were supplied with basic toiletries, she stepped back into the hospital room and opened the drawer of the dresser that faced the window so her back was to the door.

She saw a flash of light blue in her peripheral vison, the color of the hospital staff uniforms. She straightened up to see who had entered the room. Something pricked her upper arm. Almost immediately, she felt the liquid flowing through her veins.

"There now," said a low, gravelly voice she'd heard before.

She felt herself being lifted. Cloth was put

over her face, and then she was moving while she lay prone and concealed by the sheet.

She willed herself to remain conscious even as the drug caused her awareness to slip away.

The last thought she had was that she was going to die. An image of Zoe floated through her mind right before everything went black.

Neil was awake when Agent Ferris entered the room. He was groggy from all the medication he'd been given. He'd heard the agent outside his room asking the medical staff questions. It didn't sound like he wasn't getting many answers.

"Is everything all right with Arielle?"

"Actually, she's concerned about you. She said you had some kind of emergency last night."

"Not sure what happened. I was convulsing and throwing up. The nurse thought it was a reaction to an overdose of a drug. I had excessive amounts of the painkillers in my system. The nurse who administered the IV solution swears she double-checked the amount."

Agent Ferris stepped a little closer to the hospital bed. "So it could have been sabotage?"

"I suppose someone could have put something in my IV while I was passed out."

"But you're on the mend? Arielle is asking for a status report."

"Is she okay? Why can't she ask me herself?"

"She was admitted to the hospital as well. Blow to the head and back."

Neil stared at the ceiling. "The guy came after her at my place after he shot me?"

"Look, I need to cut to the chase. Arielle said he was here in the hospital last night. Left behind a threatening note."

Neil's head cleared, and he sat up straighter. He rubbed the stubble of beard growth on his chin trying to process what the agent was asking.

"I'll let Arielle know you can talk." Agent Ferris left the room.

Neil drew his attention to the movement in the hallway. An orderly pushed a gurney with a sheet over a body. A moment later, a nurse walked by headed in the other direction.

Neil assumed that the deputy had informed his family of what had happened. They might even have come by while he was unconscious. Even if he had to rest at home, he really didn't want to spend any more time in this hospital.

When he peered through the open door,

he saw Agent Ferris rush by. He heard the agent asking questions of the medical staff that sounded urgent.

Something had happened to Arielle.

Neil pulled the covers back and swung his legs around. He had just placed his bare feet on the floor when Agent Ferris entered the room.

"She's gone, isn't she?"

Agent Ferris nodded. "She would have come by if she was going to check herself out. She needs a ride."

An image clicked in his head. He ran out into the hallway, dragging his IV with him.

The nurse came toward him. "Sir, do you think you are up to walking around?"

"Was there a death in this hospital recently?"

"No. It's a small hospital—I would know."

Panic made his throat tight. Neil turned to face Agent Ferris. "He took her out on a gurney." Neil pointed down the hallway.

Agent Ferris hurried down the hallway.

Neil pulled his IV out. He couldn't get around dragging that thing with him.

"Sheriff Cobain," the nurse said.

"I don't have time for this. A woman has probably been kidnapped, and her life is in danger."

Neil knew that security for the hospital consisted of one older man who was not in good shape. All the same, he needed any help he could get. "Tell Willard to be looking for a man dressed like medical personnel pushing a gurney. Is there a way to lock the building down like department stores do?"

The nurse was already halfway across the floor. "I'll ask Willard."

"Is there some part of the hospital where someone might hide, where there isn't much traffic?"

The nurse held the phone from the nurses' station in her hand. "The old cafeteria is basically used for storage. Downstairs off the east wing."

Neil had no way to communicate with Agent Ferris. He was probably searching for Arielle, too. He didn't see him anywhere as he headed toward the elevator. He knew he was in no condition to take the stairs. The elevator opened on the older end of the hospital, which was mostly administrative offices now.

Already feeling weak from the exertion, he hurried toward where the old cafeteria was and pushed open the swinging doors. Stacked tables and chairs took up most of the space. Shelving filled with boxes lined two of the walls. There was a wall of shelving in the middle of the room that partially blocked his view.

He moved quietly across the dusty tile floor. Though he did not hear anything, he sensed that he was not alone. The swinging doors had made a noise like a soft wind when he'd come in, and he worried that if the killer was in here, it might have alerted him to Neil's arrival.

A screeching noise caused him to move faster. He ran toward the high shelf in the middle of the room and peered around, seeing only more storage shelves. There was a door at the other end of the room. He walked as fast as he could toward it. A sheet thrown on the floor set off alarm bells in his head. He peered out the tiny window that he knew looked out at the back side of the hospital. The window was murky from not being washed.

He could just make out the pond that bordered the hospital. All the air left his lungs as reached for the door handle. The killer stood over the gurney aiming Neil's gun at a motionless Arielle. He'd moved her to a place where he could make his escape quickly after shooting Arielle.

Without a thought for his own safety, Neil pulled open the door and cried out, "Hey, you."

The man was wearing a hat that covered much of his face. He raised the gun toward Neil, but then thought better of it. A pistol was only accurate at short distances. He pointed the gun at Arielle. Neil felt as though he was running down a tunnel—all he could see was the killer resting his finger against the trigger of the gun.

The killer pointed the gun and fired.

Neil cried out in anguish, kept running and braced for the inevitable.

But no explosion happened. Out of bullets. The killer tossed the gun. He glanced to where Neil was closing the distance between them.

The killer tipped the gurney so Arielle's body rolled into the pond. Neil sprinted across the field, willing his legs to move faster. The killer bolted away. Neil had no phone, no radio, no way to call for help in catching the guy, and Arielle was drowning.

As he neared the pond, he saw Arielle's body facedown in the shallow water. He took note of the direction the killer had run. He waded in and turned Arielle over so he could see her face, which was white as porcelain. She still had a pulse. When he drew her close to his ear, he could feel her breath on his cheek. Had she inhaled water into her lungs? He pulled her to shore and laid her on the grass on one side. She sputtered and spat out water. He wasn't sure if she was conscious or not. He touched her cheek. "Stay with me, Arielle. It's going to be okay."

As he stared at her lifeless face, Neil felt an ache inside that was all too familiar. Since Megan's death, he had walled off his heart. To care for someone meant risking that pain of loss all over again. He touched Arielle's cheek. "Please, be okay." The thought that went through his head, but that he could not bring himself to say out loud, was that he couldn't imagine life without her. Somehow Arielle had managed to open the passageway to his heart. He cared about her.

Neil righted the gurney and lifted her rag doll body onto it.

"Hang in there for me." When he touched her cheek, it was as cold as stone. It took some effort to push the gurney through the grass toward the sidewalk. He was still very weak from his own injuries and he feared his stitches would not hold.

He was out of breath and in pain by the time the wheels rolled across the sidewalk. He guided the gurney toward the main entrance, where he knew there would be hospital staff to meet him.

The entryway doors opened, and a nurse he didn't know greeted him.

"Oh, my. What has happened?"

"She needs medical attention. I'm not sure why, but she is not responsive. She has a pulse and is breathing. She might be drugged."

The nurse squeezed his shoulder and then stepped away to the front desk, where she called for help over the intercom. Within minutes two other medical personnel appeared, whisking Arielle away.

Completely spent, Neil collapsed in a chair. He needed to find Agent Ferris. Maybe they could still catch the killer.

A moment later, the nurse who had greeted him at the door returned.

"How is she?"

"She's in good hands." She stepped toward him. "I think we better get you back to your room."

He tried to rise to his feet but slumped back down.

"I'll get a wheelchair." She pivoted and headed down the hallway.

Neil sank even lower in the chair. He wondered if Arielle had been drugged with something or if she had sustained another blow to the head.

As the nurse pushed the wheelchair toward him, he could feel the adrenaline-fueled strength draining from his body.

He prayed that Arielle would be okay.

TWELVE

It was the sound of Zoe's voice, coming from very far away, as though in a dream, that caused Arielle to open her eyes. She was in a hospital bed. Sun shone through the slats of the blinds. Her muscles were heavy with fatigue. She struggled to keep her eyes open.

Someone stirred at the edge of the room, and then her mother was looking down at her.

"Hey, precious." Something about having her mom close made her feel safe and warm.

"I thought I heard Zoe."

"She is out in the hallway with Mary Ellen and her hubby. I didn't want her to see you unconscious—I thought it might scare her. You and Neil both have been through quite an ordeal. Your coworker brought me up to speed."

"Is Neil okay?"

"He's resting. He's the one who saved you from the pond," said Denise.

Arielle knew there was a whole story behind why she had to be pulled from a pond, but she did not have the energy for a rehash of the events that had led to her being back in this hospital bed. She could almost fill in the blanks herself from the time a needle had been jammed into her arm. The killer must have tried to drown her for whatever reason. "Just as long as Neil's okay."

Denise fluffed her daughter's pillow. "He'll recover." She leaned a little closer. "I can get Zoe if you like. She's anxious to see you."

Arielle reached up and patted her mom's shoulder. "That would be so great."

While Denise disappeared into the hallway, Arielle struggled to get into a sitting position. Images of the killer grabbing her flashed through her mind. She'd never gotten a good look at him, but his voice was distinctive. She shuddered at the memory. Once she'd lost consciousness from whatever she'd been injected with, she could not remember anything other than at one point she had heard Neil's voice telling her it was going to be okay as he held her. Had she just imagined that or had it really happened?

Like a ray of sunshine, Zoe burst into the room. "Mommy."

"Hey, ladybug."

"Let's set you up on the bed so you can be close to Mommy," said Denise.

Arielle scooted to the edge of the bed, grateful that she didn't also have to wrestle with an IV. Denise situated Zoe close to Arielle's stomach. Zoe still clung to her much-loved stuffed animal that had formerly been a rabbit.

"Good to see you, ladybug. Have you and Grandy been having fun?"

Zoe nodded. "I want to see the animals again."

Arielle reached out to stroke her daughter's arm. "I know. This whole thing has been so confusing."

Denise stood at the edge of the bed. "What if we just swung by the farm before we went back to Eric's house?"

Zoe raised her head. The look of hopeful anticipation pierced Arielle's heart. She glanced at her mother.

Denise moved closer to the head of the bed. She touched Zoe's hair and then Arielle's cheek. "Why don't you two visit for a little bit? I'll be out in the hallway, and I will come back in a few."

"Thanks, Mom."

Denise left the room. Arielle could hear

her in the hallway talking and laughing with Neil's mom.

"Grandy said you had owies." Zoe pointed at Arielle's forehead.

Arielle touched the spot where Zoe had indicated. She hadn't realized there was a bandage there, probably covering a minor scratch.

Arielle wasn't sure how much she needed to explain to Zoe. It wasn't just Zoe's physical safety she sought to protect but her emotional sense of well-being. "Yes, but I'm okay now. Mommy's going to be okay."

Zoe smoothed what was left of the fur on her stuffed animal. Arielle touched the rabbit. "Does Mr. Rabbit like where he's staying?"

Zoe held the stuffed animal close to her ear as if it was whispering something to her. It was a game that Arielle had learned to play with Zoe. Sometimes through the rabbit, Zoe could express things she couldn't quite articulate on her own.

"Sometimes he gets tired of all the new beds he has to sleep in."

Arielle thought her heart might break. "Well, we will just have to give Mr. Rabbit a big hug. Why don't the two of you come a little closer?"

She wrapped her arms around her daughter and held her close. "You tell Mr. Rabbit that soon enough he will be back in his regular bed." She held her daughter for a long, sweet moment.

Zoe pulled back and placed the worn stuffed animal close to her ear. "He says he really wants to go back to the farm and hold the little piggies and the kitties."

Arielle laughed. "Oh, is that what he says?"

Zoe nodded drawing her lips into a rosebud shape. Arielle loved the way light danced through her daughter's eyes.

Denise and Mary Ellen entered the room.

"Can Zoe come with me for a minute?" Mary Ellen stepped toward the hospital bed. "We can go get a little treat in the gift shop."

Arielle glanced at her mother and then at Mary Ellen. Clearly, some sort of plan had been cooked up between the two women. "Yes, that would be fine."

Mary Ellen gathered Zoe into her arms. "C'm'ere, pumpkin."

"Mom calls me ladybug."

Mary Ellen laughed as she gathered the child into her arms.

Denise turned and watched the other two leave the room.

"Mom, what's going on?"

Denise turned back to face her daughter.

"I think we can manage a visit to the farm, with your approval, of course."

Arielle tensed. As good as it was to see them, she worried about them even being in the hospital knowing the killer was still out there. "What did you have in mind?" All the same, she had seen how much joy Zoe got from being around the animals.

"I've already spoken to Agent Ferris. He said he could go out there with us. It would be good for Zoe to spend a little time at the farm."

"And you and Mary Ellen seem to enjoy each other's company."

"It does feel a bit like she's my long-lost sister."

She hated being in this hospital bed and feeling so helpless. "I guess that would be okay. It's really important that you make sure you're not followed."

"I know. Agent Ferris said he could escort us back to Eric's house."

"Sounds like you have thought of everything." The back of her head ached, and her body felt stiff and sore. "Wish I could go with you."

"You just rest and get better."

"I'm hoping they give me the okay to check

out later today. I really want to wrap the on-the-scene stuff up. Then we all can go home."

A shadow seemed to fall across Denise face.

Her mother didn't need to say what she was thinking. It was the same thing that was foremost in Arielle's mind. The killer was still out there. Would he follow them to Denver?

She reached out and squeezed her mother's hand. "Take lots of pictures for me."

Denise leaned over and kissed Arielle's forehead. "We're in this together."

Her mother left the room, and she rested her head on the pillow. A moment later, Agent Ferris stuck his head in the door. "How ya doin'?"

"I've been better," said Arielle. "Thank you for escorting my mom and Zoe."

"No problem." He stepped into the room so he was closer to her bed. "Listen, the real son of Betty Richards is going to be here today. He's coming in on a late-afternoon flight from Atlanta."

"I don't suppose he's staying long."

"It sounds like he's going to deal with loose ends, just the stuff he can't do remotely. He wants to leave within a day or so." Agent Ferris ran his hands through his hair. "So if we are going to do an in-person interview, it better be sooner rather than later."

"Set it up for as late in the day as he is willing to meet. I'll work on getting out of this hospital. I really want to be there. He is my last hope for unearthing some piece of evidence that kicks this investigation forward."

Agent Ferris nodded. "All righty. I'll text you with the information as soon as I get it set up. I thought we could do the interview at the sheriff's headquarters. I let Sheriff Cobain know, and he is getting his deputy onboard."

"Sounds good."

"Gotta go. I'll keep you posted about interviewing the son."

Before Agent Ferris had left the room, she was reaching for her call button. She didn't feel a hundred percent, but the hospital couldn't keep her here if she decided to check herself out. Pain shot through her when she tried to move. It didn't matter.

She needed to be at the interview. Talking to Betty's son was her last best hope for catching the Arson Killer and ending this personal nightmare.

Neil got off the phone with his deputy after arranging for the interview of Betty Richards's son and for his sheriff's car to be brought to the hospital. His shoulder hurt where the bullet had been removed. Even though he was tired and sore, he hated being confined like this. He was a man of action, and right now he was trying to figure out how they could catch this killer.

The doctor had come and gone and advised him to stay another day or at the very least rest at home. Even in his compromised state, Neil wasn't sure he wanted to do either.

His gunshot wound was evidence that the man was not above hurting someone or even killing to get to Arielle. Things had escalated quickly. He wanted to get Arielle's opinion on why that was.

Arielle stepped in his room. She was no longer wearing the hospital gown. "You're checking out, huh?"

He really didn't want to stay in this hospital. Seeing her dressed and ready to go to work only made him antsier. Neil sat up. "I just got off the phone with Greg. We are all set up for six this evening."

"We?"

"Look, I'm not staying in this hospital, and you need someone to drive you and provide some protection." He touched his good shoulder. "This is the hand I shoot with. I want to catch this guy as much as you do."

"Neil, I don't know about that. What does the doctor say?"

"When Mom and Dad came by, they told me Agent Ferris was watching over Zoe and your mom today. Greg has to be available for calls. What about the other agent?"

"He needs to go down and deal with a big case in Arizona."

"Neither of us is a hundred percent." He smiled. "Between the two of us and our injuries, we make one functioning person."

She laughed. "I do still feel kind of weak."

"Let's work on this together. I can see what kind of support I can get from my part-time guys."

"I need to go get my gun. It's locked away in one of my suitcases. I didn't want to have it out while Zoe was around. And I do need a quiet place to prep for the interview."

If she was getting her gun, she must have realized that the next time the killer came at her, she might not survive.

"I thought that guy had gotten you for sure when he came after you in the hospital."

"Mom told me what you did."

He shrugged his good shoulder.

"Thanks, Neil. I appreciate all you have done." Her voice filled with warmth.

"I haven't done enough. That guy is still out

there." The memory of holding her, looking down into that pale, lifeless face when he had pulled her from the water, flashed through his mind. He had to acknowledge that their time together had made him feel a deep affection for her. The thought of anything bad happening to her pierced him straight through.

Yet there was still a chasm between them. He hadn't broached the subject of Craig's drinking since he'd first brought it up, and it still didn't feel like he could.

"I'll let you get dressed." She moved toward the door.

"There are people out there where you are waiting for me?" The killer had gotten to her easily enough in the hospital. He might decide to come back.

She poked her head out the door. "There's a nurse at the check-in station." She gave him a backward glance and a smile. "I'll see you in a bit." She left, closing the door behind her.

With some effort, he pulled himself out of bed and walked over to where his clothes had been stored. It was painful to lift his injured shoulder to get into his shirt. By the time he was dressed, he was feeling pretty spent.

It didn't matter if he'd made a mistake in checking himself out. Arielle needed him, and he wanted to help her.

When he stepped into the hallway, Arielle rose from the chair where she was sitting and walked toward him, holding two paper coffee cups. “I got it at the kiosk around the corner. I thought we both could use a little pick-me-up.”

“Thanks.” He took the coffee.

As they made their way through the hospital, he was keenly aware of how vulnerable they were. If the killer was bold enough to come into the hospital, he would go anywhere. Neil touched his hip, where his police-issued gun ought to be.

Once he got back to his house, he had personal guns that he could grab.

He had given Greg directions on where to park his sheriff’s car. He still had his keys, and the department had a spare that Greg had used.

As they stepped out into the back parking lot, he noticed Arielle glancing around as well. She turned her attention to the high roof of the hospital.

He followed the line of her gaze.

“Were you thinking he was sitting up there with a rifle?”

“He hasn’t used the same MO twice.” She shook her head. “He keeps changing up his game, doesn’t he?”

They got to the car, and he clicked his key fob to unlock the door.

She reached for the door handle.

He stepped toward her. "Wait. Let me check under the car and inside for any sort of bomb device. Given that he keeps changing his means of getting to you, explosives might be his next choice."

When he saw the fear in her eyes, he reached out and brushed her arm.

Neil checked the undercarriage of the car and then inside. Satisfied, he nodded at Arielle while she stood some distance from the car. She climbed into the passenger seat.

Neil pulled out of the lot and headed back toward his house. As long as the killer was out there, they needed to be on high alert.

THIRTEEN

While she worked in her makeshift office, Arielle could hear Neil in the next room talking on the phone. He had taken it on himself to make sure they had video equipment in place to record the interview with Betty's son.

Returning to the house where the attack that sent both of them to the hospital had occurred brought some fear to the surface. She was glad Neil was such a calming presence. She stared at her gun in the holster where she had set it on the desk. As an agent she was required to be firearms proficient and to go to the range on a regular basis. Her job as a profiler, though, meant she mostly sat at a desk.

She looked back through transcripts and recorded interviews of key people who knew the other victims.

In all the cases, it was clear that the killer knew the victim well enough to have learned something about their habits and routines and where they lived.

Phone records showed that Betty frequently called her son. Arielle hoped he would shed some light on the questions she needed answered.

Neil popped his head in. "Are you hungry?"

"Starving."

"I can put something together in a few minutes. You want me to bring it to you while you work?"

She checked the time. They still had three hours before the interview. "No, I could use a break. I'll come out and eat with you. Let me just wrap this up."

She jotted down some final notes and then joined Neil in the kitchen. He had placed two plates with chips on them at the counter and had something spinning around in the microwave.

"Hope you like ham and Swiss."

"Sounds delicious." She wandered over to the front window. In addition to the sheriff's car, a battered old truck was parked outside. The man behind the wheel waved at her.

"That's my part-time deputy Lee. I thought we could use the extra protection given our current shortcomings." Neil placed a sandwich on one of the plates and then put the one sitting on the counter in the microwave. "I like it when the cheese is all warm and melted."

She stepped back toward the counter. "That sounds delicious." She waited until his sandwich was warmed up as well.

"I can say grace if you like," Neil said.

She bowed her head.

"Lord, we thank you for Your unconditional love and protection. We ask that You nourish our bodies with this food, and we thank You for it."

She raised her head and opened her eyes. When she looked at Neil, the softness in his expression drew her in. She lifted her sandwich and took a bite.

She brushed away some melted cheese from her mouth. "That's really good."

"Oh, I almost forgot." He retreated to the refrigerator and returned with a Ball jar. "Mom's homemade pickles."

Using a fork, he drew one out and set it on her plate. "Did she make those from cucumbers she grew?" She took a bite, enjoying the bread-and-butter flavor.

Neil nodded. "Yeah, it's kind of a lost art form."

"My mom used to do that kind of thing before she became Zoe's full-time caregiver," Arielle said.

"Maybe when Zoe is a little older, she'll be able to do that kind of thing again."

"That prayer you prayed just now. Thanking God for His protection. Sometimes it doesn't feel like He's protecting us. It certainly hasn't felt that way these last few days."

"I get that. Fifteen years ago, the woman I was going to marry died." He moved the food around on his plate for a moment before speaking up. "I'm sure you wondered why Craig's life wasn't spared."

Mentioning Craig caused a tightness in her chest, but maybe they needed to talk about this. "I've asked God that a thousand times. And your deputy told me about your fiancée dying."

"Protection looks different to us this side of Heaven. Sometimes it seems we think we are entitled to a life without suffering and loss, but in fact what makes us draw closer to God is desperation and confusion."

"Yes, I think, too, we have to allow for some mystery where God is concerned." If anyone understood some of what she had been through, it was Neil. "I appreciate what you said about Craig. It does explain why he changed so much right before he died. It was just a hard truth to take in."

"Even with the drinking problem, I could tell that he was a good agent."

"Thank you for saying that." She set her sandwich down and nibbled on the chips and pickle.

"So after this interview, you're going to be wrapping things up here?"

What was that emotion she detected in his tone? Just a slight wavering of his voice. "There is no reason after that to stay. We've gathered all the crime scene evidence we can. Now it's for me to comb through the reports."

"Makes sense."

Was it sadness she heard in his voice? "Things will be easier for Mom and Zoe once we get back home." If she wasn't able to catch him, would the killer follow her to Denver?

Neil reached over and covered her hand with his. "I guess I wanted to be the one who helped catch that guy so you don't have to be looking over your shoulder all the time."

The warmth of his touch seeped through her. She looked into his eyes, feeling a spark between them. "I wish that, too." Relishing the moment, she didn't move her hand away.

He was the first to pull away and break the power of the moment. "Would you like some tea to wash down that sandwich?" He stepped toward the refrigerator. "Can't believe I didn't think of that."

His nervousness made her smile. It wasn't just the geographic distance she'd traveled since leaving Denver, but she saw now God's hand in bringing her back to where Craig had died. What Neil had shared had answered questions and brought a degree of closure.

He poured tea from a carafe and set it on the counter for her. She took the glass. "Aren't you going to have some?"

"I think I saw Lee pull out of the driveway a while ago. I might go do a quick perimeter search of the house."

"Okay, I'd like to get into town a little early. I could be ready in twenty minutes or so. I got my prep work for the interview done."

"Sounds good." He grabbed his gun where it was sitting by the door and stepped outside.

She crossed the room to look out the big window just in time to see him disappear around the corner of the house. Neil was a good man. She was going to miss him.

Half an hour after he'd checked the perimeter and found nothing amiss, Neil and Arielle were headed to the sheriff's office. They spoke very little on the drive into town. The silence caused him to wrestle with his own feelings. He felt a deep connection to her, but they were from two different worlds, and she would be returning to hers soon.

He parked and they stepped inside. No one was inside, but Greg had left a note saying he had set up the recording equipment in the interview room.

"I'm going to go see how Greg set things up," she said.

Neil sat down at his desk and opened the notebook that each officer wrote in at the end of his shift. The log was something Neil had instituted when he'd been elected sheriff. Separate from the calls that involved legal issues and criminal acts and required a full write-up, people often called the sheriff's office about neighbor disputes and lost cats. Keeping track of those events helped Neil keep take care of the people in his county. Sometimes a neighbor complaint escalated, and if an owner had lost a dog or a cat, they needed to know that other people cared.

He was reading through the log and smiling when a door slammed, causing him to jerk and lift his head. That was either the door to the interview room or to the bathroom. He pushed his chair back and got to his feet. "Arielle?"

He stepped into the hallway and said her name again.

He thought he heard her say, "Back here," though it was muffled.

She stepped into the hallway at the same time he did. Her quizzical expression communicated that she wanted to know why he had called out to her.

"Did you hear a door slam?"

"Yes, I thought that was you."

He shook his head.

Her face blanched.

An explosive boom and the shattering of glass came from the main office. Neil pivoted and ran in the direction of the noise. Before he even entered the main office, the smell of smoke made him cough. Flames shot up from where the big front window had been shattered by some kind of explosive device. And then he saw flames shooting up, licking at the broken window.

Arielle was right behind him.

He ushered her down the hallway. "This way."

They hurried to the back door. When he tried it, the handle moved, but the door didn't budge. Someone had put some sort of barrier against it.

The smoke grew thicker as he led Arielle

to the bathroom, where he grabbed a cleaning cloth and wet it down. "Put this over your mouth. We're going to have to go out the front." He grabbed a cloth for himself as well.

When they stepped out of the bathroom, the smoke was so thick he could barely see. His phone was sitting on his desk. It wouldn't be long before a passerby or someone in the shops across the street saw the flames and called it in.

They dropped to the ground to avoid the worst of the smoke. He could barely see Arielle as she crawled on all fours in front of him. By the time the entered the office area, visibility was close to zero due to the smoke. He had to guess at where the front door was. He prayed it wasn't barred as well.

In the distance, he heard the fire engines and siren of the ambulance. His coughed. His eyes burned. The smoke was disorienting, and he felt dizzy. He could no longer hear Arielle. When he reached out toward where he thought she was, he felt a foot, but she wasn't moving. She must have succumbed to the smoke. He rose, hooked his hands under her armpits and dragged her toward where he guessed the door was.

He could see the flashing lights of the first responders through the smoke and broken window. The closer he got to the door, the hotter it became.

The heat was too much. Flames danced by the door.

The shouts and commands of the firefighters as they broke through was a welcome sound. An arm braced him and guided him through the smoke.

"There is a woman in there on the floor." Though he thought he was yelling, his words seemed to fade as he spoke them. The thick smoke rolled out the window. Whatever kind of incendiary device it was, it was designed to produce more smoke than flames.

He was led to the ambulance and given oxygen. He wheezed and had to pull the mask away from his face to cough. His lungs burned.

The firemen were hosing down the front of the sheriff's office. Through the smoke, he saw Arielle being carried and placed on a stretcher, where she was given oxygen as well. She remained motionless while an EMT hovered over her.

Across the street at the pawnshop and apartment building, people gathered on the street to watch the action.

By the time the fire was contained, Arielle

had regained consciousness. She sat up, still wearing the oxygen mask.

Neil knew most of the firemen by name. Several of them came over to see if he was okay. Arielle recovered enough to hop off the stretcher and sit beside him. They sat close together, their shoulders touching. Neither of them had the energy to speak.

The fire trucks pulled out of the parking lot. The people across the street went back inside.

One of the paramedics, a twenty-year-old named Joe Sizemore, approached Neil and crouched so he was at the same level.

"Sir, if you like, we can transport you two to the hospital. You should probably be checked out by a doctor."

Neil pulled his oxygen mask away from his face. "I think we both have had quite enough of hospitals."

Arielle nodded. "If you could just give us another few minutes to recover."

Joe nodded, patted Neil's shoulder and walked away.

Neil stared at the sheriff's building, grateful that cinder block was pretty fireproof. The smoke damage would make the place uninhabitable until they could get a crew in there to deal with smoke damage and window replacement.

Agent Ferris came up the street from the hotel four blocks away. Pulling the oxygen mask off, Arielle rose to her feet.

"I got word of the excitement down here and saw the smoke."

"We need to reroute Betty's son. Is there a place in the hotel we can do the interview?"

Agent Ferris glanced at his watch. "His plane should just be landing. I can find a spot and let him know to meet us there. Maybe there's a conference room or something."

Neil got to his feet and came to stand beside the two agents. He leaned a little closer to her. "Are you sure you're up to this?"

She coughed and took another intake of oxygen. "It's not optional."

While he appreciated her determination, he wasn't so sure either of them was up to the task.

FOURTEEN

Less than an hour later, Arielle sat in a small conference room. Luke Richards, Betty's son, had taken a chair on the other side of the table. Neil stood by the door.

Though she smelled like smoke, there had not been time to go back to Neil's and change. Instead she had gotten clothes from a little boutique and used baby wipes to get the smell off her skin.

Agent Ferris and Neil had borrowed some video-recording equipment from the high school. The sheriff's office was an official crime scene and off-limits.

Arielle stared down at the piece of paper where she'd tried to replicate her interview notes from memory. She still had not fully recovered either physically or emotionally from the fire.

She began with the most noninvasive questions, knowing that always helped the interviewee relax. The benign questions also helped her get a read on the person she was trying to gain information from. The man had just lost his mother, and she needed to be sensitive to that. After asking him questions about the flight, his job and how often he got to see his mother, she had a clear assessment of what kind of person Luke Richards was: a conscientious introvert whose life focused on his work. He was divorced with two children, and it was clear that Betty's planned visit was mostly to see her grandchildren. His flat affect about the loss of his mother could indicate a lack of connection to her, or it could be that the initial shock of the loss had not yet worn off.

She stared at her sparse notes, trying to remember what questions she had intended to ask. Once she felt she had built up some rapport and trust, she needed to draw out details that might shed light on the crime.

"Your mother's phone records indicate that she called you a day before her death. Do you remember what you talked about?"

"She wanted to give me the details about her trip. When she would land and the flight number." He looked off to the side as though he was trying to remember. "She was supposed to leave in three days. She'd had her airline ticket for months." He smiled. "She was so excited."

Arielle allowed for silence, hoping that would help bring more information to the surface.

Luke ran a hand over his bald spot and shook his head. His expression changed. Light seemed to leave his eyes as his jaw grew slack.

"I know it is hard talking about this so soon after your mother's death," Arielle said. "We want to catch the guy who did this."

"I just keep thinking, what if she had booked the flight for five days earlier. She would be hanging out with her grandkids right now." Luke glanced at the painting on the wall and then up at the ceiling. "I wouldn't be in this room talking to you. It just seems so surreal."

Arielle waited for Luke to focus his attention back on her.

Luke tapped the table and then looked at her. "I will try to help you as much as I can to figure out who did this to my mother."

"Thank you," she said. "As you know, your mother kept to herself. She didn't have a lot of friends. From what we can gather in retracing her steps, you were probably the last person to talk to her."

"Really?"

"She may have spoken to a shopkeeper or someone at the grocery store. You mother paid cash for in-town purchases, so there is no way to track her movements."

Luke rubbed his temple. "That reminds me. Mom needed spending money for the trip. She was talking about selling some of her antiques that she didn't use anymore and some gold jewelry."

"The last time you talked to her, did she mention if she had done that?"

"She might have brought up selling stuff in one of the calls before that. The phone conversations kind of blend together."

Arielle remembered on her walk-through of the crime scene seeing the antiques and the jewelry box that contained only costume jewelry. "But you don't know if she did sell the stuff. Did someone come out to her house, maybe, to look at what she had?" Betty's purse had been consumed by the fire, so there was no way of knowing if she'd had cash in it.

"You know, I'm not sure. I just remember her mentioning that she wanted to have some fun money and to be able to buy the girls some gifts." Tears rimmed Luke's eyes. "Sorry, this is all of a sudden hitting me really hard." He swiped at his eyes. "Wow, I didn't expect to get so emotional. We weren't that close."

"We can take a break if you like."

"Thanks." Luke pushed his chair back. "I just need to go splash some water on my face, take a deep breath. I want to help. I really do."

Arielle's mind was already spinning. She waited until Luke left the room before talking to Neil. "We need to look at those phone records to see if she called someone who would buy antiques or gold jewelry. They might have seen her in the hours before she died."

"Did one of your agents go through the call log and match the numbers to a name?"

"Yes, but I wasn't looking specifically for an antique place. A jewelry store could have bought the gold jewelry."

"We don't have a jewelry store, just a pawnshop. The nearest antique place is over in Wilsaw, thirty miles up the road."

"A pawnshop wouldn't give her the best price, so maybe she drove somewhere for that, too."

Luke returned, and Arielle completed her questions. Even though nothing more significant came to light, Arielle jotted a few notes. Sometimes something that didn't seem to matter at all initially turned out to be the thing that broke the case open.

Luke thanked Arielle and then left. Neil moved to get the memory card that contained the recording of the interview.

Though she wasn't sure why, the interview had energized her. "We need to go back to your house. I want to look at the timelines I constructed of the other victims' final days and go over the interviews of people who saw them last."

"Okay, why don't we grab a pizza for later on the way out of town? I don't have much food at the house."

Arielle really wanted to get back to her files, but she couldn't think straight on an empty stomach. They got into the car. Neil dropped off the recording equipment they had borrowed and then wove through town to a building that she never would have guessed was a pizza place. It looked like a house that had been converted to a restaurant. Arielle opted to go inside with Neil. She always needed to assume that she had a target on her back.

The restaurant had only two tables, so they must mostly do takeout. Neil put in his order and joked with the waitress named Missy. She liked the way he knew everyone and always took the time to connect with them. There was something to be said for living in a small town. Twenty minutes later they had their pizza.

It was getting dark as they left the outskirts of town. The aroma of the pizza wafted up from where it sat on Arielle's lap. "Smells good."

Neil turned down the road toward his house.

The cameras were still in place, and there was no sign of anyone breaking in. Once Neil cleared the perimeter, they entered together.

Neil clicked the dead bolt on the front door into place and then turned to face her. "Wait here. I'm not taking any chances. Let me make sure the whole house is clear."

Arielle placed the pizza box on the counter and pulled her gun from its holster. "I'm not a total damsel in distress. It's been a while since I've done it, but I can clear a room, too."

"Great, I'll do my room and the bathroom. You clear the hallway and the office."

Once both of them were satisfied that the house was secure, Neil got them each a plate. She grabbed a slice. "If you don't mind, I need to get to work right away."

"Do what you got to do."

Taking her pizza with her she turned down the hallway and sat down to work, pulling up computer files that contained timelines and interview transcripts. She took nibbles of the pizza while she worked, wiping her fingers on the napkin she'd grabbed.

After about ten minutes, Neil stood in the doorway. "Can I help?"

"Yes, as soon as I get these printed off. We need to go through them with a fine-tooth comb. The male victim who died in your county over two years ago…" She hurried over to the printer and scanned the interview as the printer pushed out the pages.

"What about him?"

"I seem to remember that one of his friends we interviewed mentioned that he had an antique motorcycle he wanted to sell." She scanned the interview. "It was an offhand comment. It's probably buried in the transcript."

"What do you need me to do?"

She went back to the laptop and opened up a file. "These are the reconstructed timelines of all the other victims. If you could go through these and look for any mention of the victims trying to sell something of value."

Neil sat at the laptop.

"If it's not in the timeline or the interviews, we might have to make some calls and see if we can jog the memories of the people close to the victims. I know it's a long shot. The first murder took place almost seven years ago."

Neil glanced at the time on the computer. "It's almost nine now. If you do make some calls, with the time change, you might be getting some people out of bed."

"I didn't realize it was so late." Arielle looked up from the document she was studying. "I need to call Mom and Zoe." She stood up.

"You seem excited."

"I'm hopeful that I have found the key to who this killer is. This might be the connection between all the murders I've been looking for. It narrows down who the killer could be—someone with an expertise in antiques, an appraiser or store owner. Such a suspect would know where each of the victims lived, probably chatted with them and got to know their habits and vulnerabilities. Maybe he had even been to their homes."

Arielle grabbed her phone and headed down the hallway into the living room. She couldn't wait to hear Zoe's voice. She pressed in her mother's number and stared out the window while it rang.

She stepped away from the window, realizing how vulnerable she was standing in front of it. They were getting closer, but the killer was still out there.

As Neil combed through the interview transcript, he could hear Arielle laughing while she spoke to her daughter. He winced when he lifted his injured arm. He still wasn't feeling like his old self.

When he was eating his pizza in the kitchen, he'd called his part-time deputy to see if he could swing around. Charlie, who also owned a ranch, was busy but would try to do a check-in via text. Greg had promised to do at least one drive-by patrol while on shift.

Neil focused his attention back on the computer screen. He'd gone over this interview—a close friend of the third victim, who had been killed in Bend, Oregon—twice. He could see no mention that the victim had intended to sell anything in the days before his death. He had already tried typing in some keywords in the find feature: *antique*, *sell*, *appraise*, *value*. Still nothing.

He moved to the first victim, a man in California.

Arielle popped her head in. "Anything?"

"Not yet. How are Zoe and your mom doing?"

She placed her phone on the desk and sat back down. "She had a good time at the farm. I think they are getting anxious to be back home."

"I'm sure you are, too." He hadn't expected such intense emotion to creep into his voice. "I've enjoyed working with you. Despite the circumstances."

"It's been good for me, too." He liked the way she looked at him, the softness in her eyes. "You have a nice life here."

He nodded. "Wouldn't trade it for anything."

She broke the connection of the moment, turning her attention to a page on one of her files. "I'm hoping to at least have a strong lead on the Arson Killer case before this night is over. It was one of my first cases when I took the transfer into the behavioral unit."

He looked back at the computer. "Did you put together any sort of general profile of each victim? Something that lists hobbies and work history?"

She got up and stood over the laptop, tapping the keys. "I haven't looked at those files in a while."

Neil could smell her perfume. His heart

fluttered when she stood so close to him. She pressed another button, and a new set of documents came up on the screen.

He opened the one for the first victim, Henry Vichard. He scanned it, finding the usual stuff: Henry worked as an engineer, divorced, two kids. It was on his list of hobbies that Neil stopped. “Hobbies include model railroad and collecting antique watches. Some of those watches can be pretty valuable.”

“Good job,” she said.

After three more hours of combing through documents, they discovered that four of the five victims were linked to desiring to sell or at least owning an item that would require contact with an appraiser or someone who had knowledge about the value of the items or might buy them.

Arielle yawned. “Let’s make a list of all the possible places our suspect might be working within a fifty-mile radius of the crime scene. I think we need to visit each one in person.”

“It’s almost midnight. You must be tired.”

“Sorry, I get excited when I have a break like this.”

“Why don’t you sleep in my room and I’ll crash on the couch?”

“You are probably in way more pain than

me. I'm sure sleeping in your own bed would be the best thing."

He nodded, appreciating her consideration.

Neil grabbed a pillow and blankets from the storage closet. When he entered the living room, the windows were rattling from what looked like an impending storm.

He double-checked that all the windows and doors were locked. The cameras he had set up didn't show anything to be alarmed about other than a raccoon who scurried by to get out of the rain.

Though he was extremely fatigued, he wasn't totally comfortable just going to sleep. Before going to sleep, he set his alarm to do a perimeter check in four hours.

When the alarm went off, it took him a minute to respond. After hitting the alarm button, he got up, still in his street clothes. He grabbed his holster and pulled the gun out. The pain pill had worn off. He checked the exterior cameras on his phone. It looked like the storm might have knocked one down, giving him a view of the ground by his back door.

Retreating to his bathroom, he took a pain pill before entering the living room and treading softly past a sleeping Arielle. He checked all the doors and windows again. The rain came down in gray sheets, obscuring much of his view when he glanced out the windows that faced the backyard and the forest beyond.

He reentered the living room, where the blaze of headlights filled the window. Heart racing, he shook Arielle awake.

"Wake up. Get down low on the ground."

Arielle rolled off the couch. Reaching up, she grabbed her gun from where she'd placed it on the side table.

Gripping his weapon, Neil crouched and eased toward the window.

FIFTEEN

Though she had reacted quickly to Neil's command, Arielle was still trying to shake off the fog of sleep. The headlights illuminated the whole window. Their height indicated that it was probably a truck.

"Are you sure that's not one of your guys coming to check on us?"

She was grasping at straws. If it was someone coming to check on them, why do something so overt and so menacing?

"Can't take chances. Not my guys' usual routine."

Unless of course the truck was meant to be a distraction. "Can you tell if there is even anyone in the cab of that truck?" She had a sinking feeling that perhaps the killer was trying to break in through the back door or some window while their attention was on the truck.

Neil crouched by the window, peering

above it for only a second. "It's hard to see anything. The lights are so bright I can't even tell what model car it is."

"I'm going to go check the security of the rest of the house." Still crouching, she moved toward the hallway. "What if he's trying to get in some other way?"

"No, Arielle, wait." He pulled his phone out. "Greg said he'd come by. Let me see if that is him."

"Wouldn't they have told you they were coming by to do a check?"

Neil didn't answer her. Instead he pressed a button. Someone on the other end of the line answered right away. "Is that you in the yard?"

The response was muffled.

"Really. What is your ETA?" Neil lifted his head above the rim of the windowsill. "I see you."

A window shattered somewhere in the house just as a second set of headlights appeared at the end of the driveway. That must be the deputy showing up.

"He's out there." She guessed at which window the killer had thrown an object through, maybe Neil's bedroom.

Neil rushed across the floor. "I'm going out

to see if I can catch him before he gets to his vehicle." He threw open the door.

Arielle was pretty sure it was Neil's bedroom window that had been shattered. She hurried in that direction. When she entered the room, the wind coming through the broken window swirled around her. A large rock lay on the carpet.

What was the killer hoping to accomplish by doing this? Another distraction?

After she saw Neil go by and head into the forest, she ran back into the living room.

A knock on the front door made her jump.

"Arielle, it's Greg. Neil asked me to stay with you."

She stepped toward the door and opened it.

Outside she could see both vehicles, with their headlights turned off. She let the deputy in. Greg must have turned the lights off in the suspect's truck.

"It looks like once he realized he couldn't get back to his truck with me in the driveway, he ran. Neil is going to try to catch him."

"I should go help him. He's in no condition to run very far."

"He said you might do that. You really need to stay put. If the suspect's intent is to kill you, this whole game with the headlights might be an attempt to lure you outside. He could be waiting in the trees."

Neil's judgment was sound, but she hated feeling like she was on the sidelines. She needed to do something to occupy her mind. "He broke a window as a parting gift," said Arielle. "The rain is getting in. Do you know where Neil keeps his duct tape?"

Greg shrugged.

She moved into the kitchen. The third drawer she opened was a junk drawer with a roll of duct tape.

The door flew open, and Neil stepped inside, soaked and out of breath. "I saw him, but I wasn't able to keep up with him."

Greg walked toward the door. "Which way did he go? I'll put a call in to Charlie. We can search the roads. He's on foot, so we might be able to catch him."

Neil leaned against the wall. "I'll help you with the search."

"Why don't you stay here? He might try to come back for that truck. It would just be too easy for him if no one was here to stop him."

The deputy must have seen how spent Neil was from the chase and was giving him an easy out.

Arielle said, "Neil, why don't you sit down?"

The deputy was already headed toward the

door. She grabbed a towel from the kitchen. Neil collapsed into a living room chair.

She handed him the towel and sat on the edge of the sofa so she could face him. "I know your wound was not deep. But for most people it takes weeks to recover from being shot."

Neil wiped his face. "I just thought I could catch him so this whole thing would be over for you. I'm going to go change out of these wet clothes." He put his phone on the side table. "Let me know if Greg sees anything."

She picked up the towel. "I'll watch. Greg is right that he might try to double back to get his car." It was strange that he had turned on the headlights. Was it meant to blind them with the intense light or to be an intimidation tactic?

"Turn off all the lights so it looks like no one is here."

Neil moved toward his bedroom. She hurried around the living room, clicking off the lamp and the kitchen light before taking up a position where she had a view of the abandoned car but was covered in shadow.

The porch light remained on and provided a partial view of the car.

Neil's phone buzzed. The text was from an unknown number.

Can't find him on foot. Heading back to my truck. Will search roads before heading to get some shut-eye.

Neil returned dressed in jeans and a T-shirt. "Anything?"

"Greg should be back in a minute to get his truck. He couldn't find the guy. He's going to keep searching by car for a bit more."

Neil pointed toward the window. "We should keep vigil, then. You want to rest for a while? I'll wake you up in a few hours."

"I don't know if I can fall asleep after all that excitement." Though the initial adrenaline rush had worn off, she was still wound up.

"We'll keep watch together, then. If he does come back, it might take both of us to catch him."

The killer might try breaking into the house again. Neil must be thinking the same thing, because he picked up his phone and checked the feed on the cameras, using his hand to shield the glow of the phone from being seen through the window.

"I guess we wait and we watch," she said.

Neil awoke with a start when the warmth of the sun streaming through the window hit his eyes. Though he'd dozed off and awakened through the night, he'd only been asleep for less than twenty minutes this last time.

The killer's car was still in his driveway. Arielle had fallen asleep in the chair where she'd been watching. Neil checked his texts. Greg said he hadn't had much time to search, as he had gone out on several early-morning calls.

As soon as the businesses were open, Neil would make arrangements for the car to be towed and for a forensics unit to go over it. His guess was it was stolen.

Neil's house was five miles outside town. He pushed himself to his feet. Was the guy still watching his place from some unseen vantage point?

Arielle looked at the clock on the wall. "We need to get ready. I'm going to get freshened up and grab my laptop. You can tell me off the top of your head which businesses might deal in antiques and appraisals."

Arielle seemed to be one of those people who could go from zero to sixty when she woke up. She was instantly alert, showing no sign of grogginess.

"Don't you want some coffee or something?"

"Sure." She was already halfway down the hallway, headed toward the guest bathroom.

He shook his head. After making arrangements for the car to be picked up, he turned his attention to the kitchen and preparing coffee. He had already made a mental list of the places that might lead to some connection to the serial killer. It wouldn't take long to write them down.

By the time the coffee was brewed, Arielle returned, holding her laptop and a piece of paper. She had braided her long brown-sugar hair and changed her clothes. She set the piece of paper on the counter.

He pulled the lid off the sugar container. "How do you like your coffee?"

"Just a little sugar."

He set the steaming mug of coffee and the sugar bowl in front of her, along with a spoon.

Neil poured himself a cup, grabbed the piece of paper and started to make a list. There was an estate auction warehouse about seven miles outside town, the pawnshop in town, a man he knew did appraisals who lived in Silver Creek and an antique shop in a town twenty miles away. All might provide some leads.

Arielle took a sip of her coffee and tapped the keys on her laptop. She looked at the list

Neil had made and added one more to it. "I kept it within a fifty-mile radius of where Betty and the other victim died. We may have to expand that search if nothing turns up."

By the time they finished their coffee, the tow truck had shown up for the car. After they locked everything up, they stepped outside into the morning sun.

As the tow truck pulled away, Neil noticed Arielle studying the trees that surrounded his house. "Where do you suppose he's gone?"

Neil shook his head as they climbed into the sheriff's vehicle. "Hard to say. Where do you want to go first?"

Arielle looked at the list. "I suppose the pawnshop in town is the closest."

"They don't open for another hour. The guy who does appraisals and the estate auction warehouse would be the next closest."

"Then I guess that is what we'll do."

Neil drove down the country road that led to a paved two lane. Though he had not interacted much with the man who did appraisals, Neil knew Ralph Ingram by sight and by what other people had told him. He was in his late fifties, a widower who had moved here from another state about some years ago. "This guy is in good shape but older, so he might be ruled out because he lacks the physical strength that you said was part of the profile."

Arielle stared out the window. "Why does this area look familiar to me?"

"Ralph's house is in an adjoining subdivision not far from where Betty lived." He found himself checking the rearview mirror as he drove. The only thing that made him more nervous than an assault from the killer was when nothing had happened for a long time. It concerned him that something big might be just around the corner.

"Proximity would create opportunity," she said.

Neil rolled through a subdivision where the lots were much smaller than the one Betty had lived on. "He's retired, so he travels some, and I know he goes south for the winter."

"More opportunity to commit the other murders."

Neil realized that if Ralph was involved with the murders, he might make a run for it when he saw the sheriff's car. He doubted he would take off on foot, but he might try to escape in a car.

When he pulled up to the house, there wasn't a car parked by it. The garage door was shut. He didn't see any sign of life in the house. No one came to the window to peer out.

He and Arielle got out. His hand brushed over his gun. "I'll let you ask the questions. If you get any red flags, we can officially take him in for questioning. If he is involved, I don't want to give him a chance to flee."

Arielle seemed to be taking in the surroundings as they made their way up the sidewalk to the house. Just as she reached up to knock on the door, he wondered if there was a back door and if Ralph would try to leave that way.

She knocked. No answer.

"I'm thinking maybe I better check around back." The garage was connected to the house. Although running would make him look guilty, Ralph could escape that way in a car.

A middle-aged woman in a floppy hat holding tulip bulbs came out from the back of her house. She leaned on the fence that separated the two properties. "Are you looking for Ralph, Sheriff?"

"Yes, ma'am."

"He went on some trip or other. Left this morning. Asked me to pick up his mail and water his plants."

None of this looked good for Ralph. That would have meant he was in town at the time of Betty's murder, and he could have been at his house just a few hours ago.

Arielle stepped toward the fence. She flashed her badge. "I'm Special Agent Olson with the FBI."

"You're here because of what happened to that poor woman. That fire was something else. I saw the smoke from my house." The woman brushed her forehead and leaned on the fence. "You don't think Ralph had something to do with that?" Her tone had become gossipy.

"We're just making inquiries at this point. Do you know if Ralph knew the victim?"

"She was never at his house that I know of. I saw her picture in the paper...poor lady."

Neil walked closer to the two women. "How long is Ralph going to be gone?"

"He requested I pick up his mail for five days."

"Can you give us a call when he comes back?"

The neighbor narrowed her eyes as suspicion crept into her voice. "Sure, I can do that."

Neil hoped the woman would not tip off Ralph, giving him an opportunity to disappear.

If Ralph was their guy and he had truly left town, at least the attacks would stop. Even though Ralph was high on the list of suspects, he didn't totally fit the profile. It made sense to check out the other businesses. Neil and Arielle got back in the car and drove to the second place on their list, a warehouse for an estate auction place.

The address was outside town, not far from the private landing strip where they had encountered the killer. The warehouse consisted of two barns next to a house. A sign at the top of the driveway indicated they were at the right place. A knock on the door of the house revealed that no one was home. There was a car parked by one of the barns.

"Maybe somebody is in there."

They walked the short distance to the first barn, where the car was parked. The large barn doors were open, and they could hear noise coming from inside. The barn held high shelves stacked with every object imaginable—car parts, record players, books, musical instruments.

The noise was coming from behind one of the shelves. Whoever it was, it sounded like he or she was sorting and moving something.

Neil called out. "Hello, we're looking for the owner of Breyer Estate Auctions or someone that might answer some questions for us."

"What do you need? I don't own the place. I just work here. Maybe I can help you."

Neil was about to identify himself as the sheriff when Arielle gripped his hand.

Her words came out in a frantic whisper. "That voice. I know that voice."

He heard footsteps, and the man popped his head out from one of the tall shelves. Shock spread across his face when he saw Arielle and Neil. He darted for the door.

"It's the killer," she said.

Both of them ran toward the open door just as the man's car started up and sped out of the driveway.

They sprinted the short distance to the sheriff's car, which was parked by the house. The suspect had a bit of a head start on them.

He took note of which direction the guy had turned once he was at the end of the driveway.

Neil pressed the gas and headed up the tree-lined country road where the other car had gone. He lifted his radio and pressed the talk button. "Greg, I need some backup. Suspect in a blue Tahoe headed eastbound on Old Culver Road."

Greg's voice came over the radio. "Roger

that. I'll get to the crossroads where he might come out at as quickly as I can."

Neil put the radio down. He glanced at Arielle, who was still white as a sheet.

SIXTEEN

Arielle's breathing was shallow as she tried to sort through her racing thoughts and quell the rising fear. She had just looked into the face of the killer she'd been chasing for years. She guessed that he was maybe forty, but the long hair made him look younger. The emptiness in his eyes that scared her the most, signs of a man with no conscience.

Neil maintained a steady speed as the blue Tahoe disappeared around a tree-lined curve. In a halting fashion, Neil responded as if he was trying to put ideas together as well. "This guy…is guilty of something…or we wouldn't be chasing him, right? I saw the shock on his face when he saw us."

"It's him. He had the same voice as the man who tried to kidnap and kill me."

The road became even curvier as the Tahoe slipped in and out of sight. Arielle's mouth had gone dry and she felt light-headed.

Neil stared straight ahead. They hadn't seen the Tahoe for a few minutes.

Greg's voice came across the radio. "No sign of him here."

Neil picked up the radio. "We lost him, too. Can you stay in place awhile longer? I'm thinking he may have turned off at that fishing access."

Greg responded in the affirmative.

Neil found a wide shoulder and turned around.

She pulled out her phone. "It will be easy enough to find out the name of the guy we are chasing. He's employed by the estate auction company."

"If he used his real name." Neil hit his blinker when the fishing access sign came into view. The Tahoe was parked by the river, and the driver's-side door was flung open.

They were dealing with a fugitive at this point.

Neil got back on the radio and explained the situation to Greg, advising him that he needed to round up at least one of the part-time deputies. "If he's traveling on foot at this point, my guess is he'll try to get to a road."

Neil stopped the vehicle about ten yards from the abandoned vehicle.

Neither of them moved. Except for the

breeze that shook the top of the trees, a stillness fell around them.

Arielle put her phone away and leaned closer to the windshield. "Do you think he's still in his car, waiting to get at us?" She'd have to call the estate auction owner later.

Neil shook his head. "Why leave the door open like that? I think he jumped out and hid in a hurry." Neil scanned the entire area, and then his gaze landed across the river. "I also think that he's not going to give up and just take off running. He had a better chance of escape in the car."

Arielle gripped the armrest. "He's setting us up. Staging a scene so we'll move in. He's probably armed."

Neil had already shifted into Reverse when the first shot was fired.

It must have gone through one of the tires, because the car lurched and jerked.

Neil kept backing up the road. "We have to take cover and get him before he gets us. He's not going to go back to that car if he thinks he'll get caught. We can hold him off so he has to flee on foot."

He turned the wheel so the car was sideways to the road. Another shot was fired. It made a pinging noise as it glanced off the body of the car.

She studied the trees where the shot seemed to have come from. "I think he's over there."

"We need to bail through the driver's side." Neil opened the car door. He got out and crouched low, working his way to the hood of the car where he could watch.

Arielle's heart pounded against her rib cage. She slid down lower, so her eyes were barely above the dashboard as she inched across the seat. She glanced through the windshield, well aware of what a target she was when she lifted her bottom a little higher to get over the console between the bucket seats. Her teeth pressed together as she braced for the passenger-side window to shatter.

Her gaze focused on the cluster of evergreens where the last shot had come from. She detected no glint of metal from the rifle or movement of any kind. A man on foot would be easy enough to catch as long as he didn't acquire another car or have help in getting away.

She crawled out of the car, taking up a position by the back bumper. As the seconds ticked by, her glance moved from the car to the trees.

She theorized that the suspect would try to run back to the Tahoe and escape if he thought he had a chance of getting away.

If they could impound the Tahoe and get a forensic unit to go over it, it probably held a wealth of information. Even if the name on the registration was fake, there was probably DNA all over that car. If this was her killer, he had probably used the stolen black truck because the Tahoe could be linked back to him as his personal vehicle.

"I don't think he's going to give up super easy and just take off running. He probably wants to access that car."

"Agreed." Neil moved back toward the open door of the police car. "I'm going to see if we can get more help and a functioning car here." He reached for his radio.

Another shot split the silence. She winced and moved away from the edge of the car.

As Arielle scanned the area around the Tahoe, all she could hear was Neil's muffled voice while he talked on the radio.

The suspect burst out of the trees and fired another shot at them, then fell to the ground.

"Neil, he's making his move."

They both only had handguns. In order to have any accuracy at all, they would have to move in closer.

The suspect leaped up and then sought cover behind a rock not too far from the river. He was getting closer to his car.

It was clear they needed to stop the suspect from getting his car and to hold him in place until help got here. Both of them moved in with their weapons drawn. Arielle watched as the suspect placed his rifle on the rock and prepared to aim. She and Neil dropped to the ground and crawled toward the Tahoe, seeking cover as they approached.

The rifle shot came so close to hitting her that her eardrum hurt from the sonic sound of the bullet.

Neil lifted his head. “No.” Though he whispered, his voice was filled with anguish.

Arielle looked in the direction of his gaze. Still holding the rifle, the suspect was making a run for the car. His long hair covered part of his face. Was she looking at the man who had killed five people?

Neil burst to his feet and took aim at the suspect, firing off several shots.

The man stumbled, taking cover in the trees closest to the car.

Arielle could only guess at where he was. She moved toward the car at the same time Neil did. More shots were fired, forcing them to drop to the ground. All they needed to do was hold him in place until help showed up. The slope of the land was such that as long as they remained flat against the ground, it would be a waste of a bullet to try to hit them.

If the suspect was still in the trees, he had a clean shot at them the second they stood up, and there was nothing to use as cover on the way to the car.

She lifted her chin, trying to discern where the suspect was. The long silence suggested that the guy had weighed his odds and chosen to flee on foot.

Neil looked over his shoulder, probably wondering when help would show up. He turned his head sideways so he could get her attention. They were both on their stomachs about six feet apart.

"Do you think he took off?"

"Only one way to find out," Neil said.

Her breath caught in her throat as he rose to his feet. He didn't fully straighten up for a few seconds.

She braced for shots to be fired but was met with only the sound of the wind shaking the trees.

Realizing he risked being caught, the suspect must have taken off.

"I'm going after him on foot. You stay here with the car in case he tries to double back."

"Neil, I don't think it's safe for you to go alone. What if he's just hidden deeper in the forest and is waiting for chance to shoot one of us?"

"You're his prime target." Neil had already pivoted to run toward where the suspect had gone. "Besides, someone needs to meet Greg and the other deputy when they show up." He took off running before she could respond.

But the killer had come after Neil before. He wasn't safe, either.

Arielle made her way toward the suspect's car, half expecting to hear a rifle shot behind her. She opened the passenger-side door and dug into the glove box, pulling out the car registration.

Anxiety flooded her mind when she glanced up in time to see Neil disappear into the trees. She hoped the suspect wasn't laying yet another trap.

Neil sprinted through the forest, looking everywhere for the suspect. As the trees grew closer together, he ran down the most likely path the other man had taken.

To his side, he heard the rushing of the river.

He slowed down, not certain of which way to turn. The suspect had been wearing clothes in neutral colors that would easily blend with the branches and budding trees. Neil was fully aware that the man could be positioned somewhere waiting for his chance to shoot him. He kept moving, scanning his surroundings but not seeing or hearing anything that would indicate where the other man had gone.

Neil came out by the river, and the realization hit him—the only way for the suspect to get away fast without a car would be to jump in and let the current carry him away. Neil jogged downriver, not seeing anything. The river curved in such a way that his view was limited.

He searched the forest for a few minutes more before returning to where Arielle had been joined by Greg.

The deputy stepped toward him. "We're going to get this car towed and have a forensic unit go over it. Arielle is on the phone right now with her partner, trying to get a line on the name on the car registration."

Arielle clicked off her phone and joined the other two men. "No sign of him?"

"I'm pretty sure he used the river as a means of escape."

Greg pulled out his phone. "I'll see what kind of manpower we can round up to do an intensive wilderness search."

"Maybe we can get a search-and-rescue

unit from another county involved as long as we have an officer go with them."

"I can wait here for the tow truck and ride with the driver." Greg drew his attention to the flat tires on the sheriff's car. "Looks like we're going to have to get a tow for your car as well." He handed Neil the keys. "You can take my car if you want to drive that road than runs mostly parallel to the river."

"Good idea."

He and Arielle headed toward the other police vehicle and got in.

Once they were back on the main road, Arielle pulled her phone out. "I'm going to call our suspect's employer and find out what they know about him." She stared at the phone for a moment. "Neil, what if he is the man I've been chasing all these years? I know we need to gather all the evidence, but what if he is?"

"If that is the case, then our suspect knows he's been made. He's probably going to try to flee this county as quickly as he can. He's been working here for a while at least. He might have resources, people he knows who will help him escape." Neil studied the road and tried to remember if there was some way to get even closer to the river. He waited for an opening in the forest and turned the SUV down a rough path that led them closer to the river.

Arielle spoke into her phone. "Hello, I am an agent with the FBI. Am I speaking to the owner of Breyer Estate Auctions?… Yes. I would like to ask you about one of your employees." She glanced at the registration she must have pulled out of the Tahoe. "Albert Stein… No one of that name works for you?… This man is in his midthirties, lean, long hair… I see…"

Arielle clicked a button so the phone was on speaker.

A woman's voice came across the line. "The man you're describing does work for me, but he goes by the name Aaron Phillips. He's very knowledgeable about so many of the items that we end up selling. I believe he also works part-time at the pawnshop."

That explained the attacks on the sheriff's office. The guy had a full view of who was coming and going from across the street.

"Is Aaron in some kind of trouble?"

"I can't comment on that right now. What kind of employee is he?"

"Like I said, he has wealth of knowledge about antiques, guns, old cars. He is helpful enough with clients but honestly, his love affair is with the items he handled for us."

Arielle's voice took on a faraway quality. "You've been very helpful. Do you know who Aaron's associated with, who his friends might be?"

"To be honest with you, I don't know him that well. He comes and he does his job, and he does it well. He never really talked much about himself or his personal life."

"Thank you. We may need to ask you some further questions."

"Sure, no problem."

Arielle hung up and stared through the windshield.

Neil had found a way to travel almost parallel to the river on a bumpy road. He still saw no sign of the suspect.

Arielle's words came out in a halting fashion, as though she was still trying to comprehend what she had learned. "He was more attached to things than people, not surprising. He may have financed his moves by selling objects his victims owned."

Neil studied the river. There was a long straight stretch that gave him a clear view. Perhaps they had searched enough. Because it was spring, the river was still cold. Chances were the suspect would have gotten out at the first opportunity.

"I'll see if I can get Search and Rescue involved in trying to find this guy before he puts together a means of escape."

Arielle nodded. "I'm just trying to put the puzzle pieces together here. My job is figuring out *why* criminals makes the choices they do."

Neil tensed and gripped the steering wheel even tighter. "Hopefully, we'll have some answers and a real name and can get this guy into custody."

SEVENTEEN

Arielle felt encouraged as Neil drove past the parking lot of the sheriff's office. The place was too smoke damaged to be used in any capacity. Agent Ferris had gotten a conference room in the hotel to use as the command center. There was still much work to do, but she was hopeful that before the day was over, the suspect would be in custody.

On the drive back into town, Neil had been on the phone getting several search-and-rescue teams deployed to the area where Aaron, or whatever his name was, had probably jumped into the river. The initial report was that the dogs had picked up a trail right away and figured out the exact spot where the suspect had gone into the water.

Working from scent of items in the car meant the dogs would also be able to find the point where Aaron had gotten out of the water.

Once they got to the hotel, Agent Ferris was waiting for them inside, sitting at a desk with his laptop. She had already phoned him and let him know what was going on and given him all the information about the suspect.

He looked up from his keyboard. "We're trying to work at lightning speed to figure out who this guy is. The Tahoe is parked at the impound yard behind the sheriff's office. A forensic team is on their way. I've already lifted fingerprints and put them into the system. We do know that the Tahoe was stolen from Palm Springs."

Palm Springs had been the site of one of the murders over three years ago. "If this is our guy, he probably has gone by an alias every time he settled into a town."

While Agent Ferris worked and Neil stayed in touch with the search-and-rescue teams, Arielle digested all the information she had learned in the last few hours. Their suspect was a man who loved objects more than people. Enough to kill for them? Someone like that had no doubt suffered extreme neglect. So much so that he didn't see people as a source of comfort or connection.

Neil put his phone down. "You seem a million miles away."

She shook her head. "Just trying to figure out what makes this guy tick. It will help us catch him." She needed to do follow-up interviews with the relatives who had dealt with the estates of the victims. Things like an antique motorcycle would be noticed if they were missing, but how easy would it be to steal a watch or jewelry to finance moves?

Agent Ferris jumped up from the desk where he was working. "We have a name to go with the fingerprints." He hurried toward the printer, which he must have borrowed from the hotel. Once the page rolled out, he set it in front of Arielle.

She stared down at the picture. "Why does he look familiar?"

Agent Ferris gazed over her shoulder. "He was brought in for questioning on an arson case a couple hundred miles from here. An empty warehouse caught fire. It was on federal land, so it was our case. No one died. You probably watched a tape of the interview or it at least came across your desk."

"Why was he even brought in?"

"He matched the description of someone seen around the warehouse days before. It just so happened that he got stopped by highway patrol for a broken taillight. That's why he was even on the radar. There wasn't enough evidence to tie him to the fire, though."

She studied the picture. Even in a photograph his eyes held no light or emotion. "It probably was him who started the fire, and he was no doubt practicing like arsonists sometimes do."

"I remember doing that interview. The guy was really believable. I didn't think he had anything to do with the fire," said Agent Ferris.

"I'm sure he's very convincing in an interview," Arielle said. "I also think picking him up like that made him panic. He had to do something to derail the investigation. That's why he lured us up here." She stared down at the photograph. The man looking at her had shorter hair than the one they'd seen at the estate warehouse. "Do you have a name to go with the face?"

"We think his real name Mitchell Sandburg. He's not in the system. Never been arrested unless it was as a juvenile." Agent Ferris looked at the second piece of paper he had pulled off the printer. "The guy is a total chameleon—changes his name and appearance every time he moves to a new place." He pushed the paper toward Arielle.

The printout was of a series of driver's licenses, all of the same man but with a new name and a new look. Maybe Mitchell Sandburg wasn't even his real name, but it was the one they would go with.

"Thanks for working so fast, Agent Ferris." She studied the printouts of licenses even more closely. Every single one had been issued in a location where a murder had taken place. Arielle shivered even though the room was not cold. This was the face of the Arson Killer. "We can't let this guy get away."

Neil's phone rang, and he stepped away to take the call. She caught snippets of the conversation. He was talking to one of the search teams.

Arielle turned to face Agent Ferris. "If he's not in the system, how did you manage to track him down?"

"I looked at the Facebook page for the estate auction place. He made the mistake of being in one of the photos. You can tell he doesn't want to be photographed. From there I remembered the interview."

"No wonder he was nervous about getting caught. He thought he could break me and derail the investigation," Arielle said.

Neil returned to where the two of them were sitting. She showed him the printouts and brought him up to speed. "What was the call about?"

"One of the teams was able to pick up the scent on the other side of the river, but they lost it on a two-lane road. They think he may have gotten into a car."

"Do we know where this guy was living? His employer said he'd been here for several months."

"No, but we can find out." Agent Ferris had already picked up his phone. He identified himself and explained why he needed information about the suspect. He grabbed a pen and piece of paper.

Neil sat down at his computer. "I'm looking at the satellite photos of the area where the team said they lost the scent. There are some houses around there where he may have gotten access to a car by whatever means."

Arielle stood over Neil's shoulder and stared at the satellite photos of scattered houses tucked back into the trees. "We can't let this guy leave the county. He'll disappear forever. Pop up in another county in five years doing the same horrible stuff."

Agent Ferris got off the phone. "He listed his residence as one of the apartments next to the pawnshop."

"Clearly, we'll have to get a warrant for

it, but that is not our priority right now." She suspected they would find a collection of objects he had acquired through his two jobs. "Let's catch this guy. What can we do to make that happen?"

Neil looked at the satellite photos again. "There are several directions he could have gone. This is a manhunt at this point. I'll get as many law enforcement people on it as I can. Highway patrol can set up some checkpoints. He's not getting away."

Agent Ferris looked at the map as well. "I can take this area here that connects with the highway."

"I can put Greg on the back roads south of town. He knows the area really well. Arielle, why don't you come with me?"

Both of them hurried outside. They had just gotten into a different sheriff's car when Arielle's phone rang. It was Pastor Eric's number. Her breath caught. "Hello, Eric."

"Arielle, I don't want to alarm you, but I am a little concerned. Neil did not give me any details, but he implied that there was a safety issue with your mom and Zoe."

Arielle felt as though an anvil had just been placed on her chest. She took a sharp breath between each word. "What's. Going. On?"

Neil must have picked up on the terror in

her voice, because he pulled over and pressed the brake but left the car running.

"Zoe and your mom left the house over an hour ago to go to the park, which is only a few blocks away."

A lump formed in Arielle's throat. "Is she answering her phone?"

"No, but I'm sure there's an explanation. She could have set the phone down while she played with Zoe. Peggy is walking over to the park right now to see if she can find them."

"Please stay in touch. Let me know if you find them." She looked at Neil. "We're headed that way."

Neil hit the gas and pulled out onto the road.

The road clipped by as Arielle struggled not to give in to her worst fears. "Eric said they just haven't come back from the park."

"There's lots of places they could have stopped. There's a little ice cream shop not far from the park." Neil gripped the steering wheel so tight his knuckles were white.

She knew that Neil was trying to sound reassuring. Denise might not be answering her phone because the battery had gone dead.

Ten minutes later, Arielle's phone rang. It was Eric's number, but he didn't say anything at first.

"Eric?"

"We found Denise's purse on the sidewalk. They never made it to the park."

Eric said something about contacting the local police, and then he asked to talk to Neil. Arielle didn't remember if she had said goodbye to Eric as she put the phone on speaker.

She felt like she was hearing the conversation between Eric and Neil through an auditory fog.

Neil hung up the phone. It started to rain. The windshield wipers swished across the glass. He made several calls to divert manpower to town, where Eric lived.

"We're going to get this guy. Your mom and Zoe will be okay."

"I hope that's true."

"We have to assume that he has taken them as some sort of leverage, right? He knew he probably wouldn't be able to get away this time, so he raised the stakes."

Arielle spoke as though she was on autopilot. "We won't know anything until he contacts us...if he contacts us. There still might be some different reason why they have disappeared." She simply could not process that her little girl and her mom were in the clutches of that animal.

As the lines on the highway streaked by

and she tried to clear her mind and stay calm, an unspoken prayer rose up inside her.

Oh, God, please help us. Keep them safe.

Neil's jaw clenched as they came to the outskirts of town, where Eric lived. He had nothing but dark thoughts about Mitchell Sandburg. To bring a child and older woman into his madness was beyond evil.

Arielle stared at her phone. "He hasn't contacted me yet. This might just be about revenge. He wants to hurt me because I was about to catch him. He clearly sees me as the enemy, the one who can bring his evil deeds to light and put him away, so he tried to stop me. He just keeps raising the stakes." Tears rimmed her eyes and rolled down her cheeks. "I never meant for this to happen. Mom and Zoe are my world."

Neil could not bear to see her in so much distress. He had to do something to make it better.

Neil pulled the car over. He got out and opened the passenger-side door, gathering Arielle into his arms and holding her while she wept.

Tears formed in his eyes as well. She pulled back and gazed up at him. Her hand rested on his cheek. "Hey."

His throat had gone tight with the intense emotions that raged through him. "I haven't known Zoe long, but she has a way of getting into a guy's heart."

Arielle reached up and brushed a tear trailing down his cheek away.

What he saw when he looked into Arielle's eyes was the life that had been stolen from him, the life he might have had if Megan had not died. "I just never thought I could care about a kid that much."

"It's an amazing thing, isn't it?" Her expression darkened. "I'd give my life for her to be safe. This is so wrong."

He pulled her close and held her. "We will bring Zoe and your mom home safe, no matter what it takes."

Her body shook from the intensity of her crying.

Neil kissed the top of her head. She tilted her chin so her gaze met his. He covered her mouth with his lips and kissed her deeply, both seeking comfort in each other's arms.

She rested her cheek on his chest while he stroked her hair. Though fear over Zoe's and Denise's safety lingered at the corners of his awareness, his soul was nourished and his fears tempered by being close to Arielle. They would face this together.

"Thank you for caring about Zoe so much."

He laughed and drew back so he could look Arielle in the eyes. "It's not hard to do. She's a very special little girl."

"Neil, I'm afraid. I'm really afraid." The tears flowed again.

"We should pray."

She nodded. "I can't find the words."

Pressing his forehead against hers, he closed his eyes. "Lord God, we are so scared right now. Please keep that little girl and her grandmother safe. Give us wisdom and strength to face this and to know what our next move should be."

"Amen."

Neither of them seemed to want to pull free of the hug.

Arielle finally spoke up. "I'm ready. Let's go deal with this."

Neil got back behind the wheel and drove the short distance to Eric's. Two city police cars were already parked outside. Eric and his wife, Peggy, stood on the porch talking to one of the officers. When he saw them, Eric stepped away from the conversation and walked toward Arielle and Neil.

"The local police are conducting a town-wide search," Eric said. "An Amber Alert has gone out."

"Can you take us to where you found the purse and point us toward the park? We'll start questioning people to see if they saw anything."

Eric patted Neil's shoulder. "Sure, my friend. It will be faster to walk. The park is just two blocks up and around a corner."

Arielle remained silent as they walked side by side. If this was tearing Neil apart, he couldn't imagine what it was doing to her. He wished he could hold her some more.

Eric pointed to the place on the sidewalk where he'd found Denise's purse. There were no houses close by. If anyone had seen anything, they would have been driving or walking by.

"She tossed that purse as a sign to us. My mom was married to a cop for years. Dad taught her all kinds of stuff."

"Mitchell must have taken them at gunpoint," Neil said. "How else could he have gotten away so cleanly and quickly?" From where they stood, Mitchell would have had a partial view of Eric's house. He could have been watching and waiting for them to leave.

Arielle massaged her forehead.

Neil reached out for her, rubbing her upper arm. "You okay?"

"What is he planning on doing to them?"

"The guy knows he's caught and he's getting desperate. That Amber Alert will make it even harder for him to leave the county."

"That doesn't mean Mom and Zoe will be unharmed. It could mean the exact opposite."

Neil wrapped an arm around her back and squeezed her shoulder. It did concern him that Mitchell hadn't contacted them yet with some kind of demand, but he didn't want to say that to Arielle.

"What if this is just about revenge, not making some sort of deal? He just wants to hurt me in the worst way possible. There's no telling what he will do." Arielle sounded like she might start to cry again.

Eric stood close to both of them. "I know this is close to unbearable." He gave Arielle a hug. "I think the best way I can help is to head back to the house. I'll call everyone I know, and we'll search this little town top to bottom."

"Let us know if you learn anything more," Neil said. "Maybe the city cops can pick up the trail."

"You do what you have to. Peggy and I will be back at the house. We'll be praying and making calls to get as much help as we can in place. And we'll let you know if we hear anything at all." Eric walked back up the street.

Before Eric had gotten half a block away, Arielle's phone rang. She shook her head. "I don't know this number." She pressed the talk button.

"Hello." Arielle's forehead wrinkled. "Is someone there? Who is this?"

EIGHTEEN

"Arielle?"

The voice on the other end of the line was faint. "Mom, is that you?" Arielle asked.

He mom spoke in a frantic whisper. "He's right next door."

"What do you mean? Where are you? Is Zoe..." She couldn't bring herself to ask the question.

"He's coming back. Small room, rose wallpaper, dust, doorknobs missing."

The line went dead. Her stomach had tied up into a tight ball.

Neil leaned close to her. "Arielle?" He cupped his hand on her upper arm.

She brought her trembling hand to her mouth. She could not fully process what she had just heard. "He has my mother in an old, dusty room. She said the doorknobs were missing."

Neil shook his head. “That’s all she could tell you?”

“Can they trace the call?”

“Sure, but that will take some time,” Neil said. “I think we need to figure out where she is faster than that. Did you hear any noises, or did she say anything else?”

“The wallpaper had roses on it.” Arielle shook her head. “It sounds like someplace old, abandoned.”

That could be a hundred places in the county. They did not have the time or manpower to check every one. They had to find a way to narrow it down. “Missing doorknobs, meaning they were removed?”

“Who would want old doorknobs? Why remove them?”

He had a vague memory of the estate auction place having things that looked like they had been taken out of old houses. “I wonder if that estate auction place did salvages of abandoned places. Doorknobs would be one of the things they would take.”

“I’ll call them and ask.” She stared at her phone, trying to quell the rising terror that made it hard to focus.

Neil’s voice filled with compassion. “Let me make the call.” He lifted the phone out of her hand and scrolled through until he found the number.

For Zoe, she needed to remain calm. Her mother had had the presence of mind to grab Mitchell's phone when she got the chance. That didn't mean Denise was okay. This kind of anxiety wasn't good for a woman with a heart condition.

God, help us get to them before it's too late.

Arielle listened to Neil's one-sided conversation as she struggled not panic. It sounded like they were on the right trail.

"Yes, I know where that is… Yes, thank you. You've been very helpful." He clicked off the phone and walked toward the car. "Come with me. We need to hurry." He burst into a trot, and she kept up with him.

The two city cops were no longer outside Eric's house.

Once they were in the car, he handed her back her phone. "She gave me three possible locations where they had recently salvaged old buildings. My guess is he went to the one closest to here. From the time we saw him to the time we got the call from Eric was not very long."

"Where is that?"

"A hundred years ago, there was a little town that was abandoned once the railroad didn't go through there anymore. There are still some buildings standing." Neil turned the car around and rolled toward the street. "We can't do this alone. Call Agent Ferris, Greg and anyone who can make it there quickly." He handed her his phone. "The part-time deputies, Charlie and Lee, are in my phone as well. Tell them we think he is hiding out at the Telluride ghost town. They will know where it is."

This was a hostage situation. If they were doing it by the book, a tactical team and negotiator would have been brought in. On a gut level, she knew they didn't have that kind of time. "How long does it take to get there?"

"For us, less than twenty minutes. Depending on where the others are in their search, it should take them about the same amount of time."

After Arielle made the calls, the drive on back country roads went by in a blur. Greg, Agent Ferris and Charlie all said they would get there as fast as they could and agreed to remain out of sight and just watch the place for activity if they arrived before Arielle and Neil did.

The trees that lined the road went out focus as she fought to not give in to the rising terror she felt. She pulled her phone out and stared at the screen. The second her mother saw the opportunity, she'd grabbed Mitchell's phone. The number was still on there. No doubt it was a phone the Mitchell would toss if he managed to escape.

She lifted her head. It was hard to think in the logical, free-of-emotion way she'd been taught as a profiler when the safety of her daughter and mother was concerned. "Everything Mitchell Sandburg does is calculated."

Neil glanced over at her and then turned his attention back to the road. "Yes, so what are you thinking?"

"Using arson to burn up forensic evidence, taking the job at the pawnshop so he had a view of the sheriff's offices. All of that reveals someone who is meticulous in planning his crimes."

"You also said he gets a sick thrill out of watching the fallout from the crimes he commits. So there's an emotional component."

She nodded. "It may be that his pride has been wounded because we're so close to catching him. His thinking may be distorted. Maybe he thought by killing me, the investigation would go away." It helped to talk things though with Neil. If the killer was at this ghost town, they couldn't just show up. They had to have some sort of strategy.

"Or maybe his ego is just so twisted and inflated that he saw you as an obstacle that kept him from killing."

Her throat got tight. "That's just it. People are objects to him. When they are no longer useful, he gets rid of them."

"Arielle, we will get your mother and Zoe out of this alive."

Fear gripped her heart so tight, she couldn't form the words to respond right away. "I just wonder if he left that phone where my mom could grab it on purpose to lure us there."

Neil slowed down as the road became bumpier and then turned to gravel. "We're getting close. Has anyone texted that they are in place?"

She looked at Neil's phone. "Agent Ferris is there. And the other two are within five minutes."

"Ask Agent Ferris where he parked."

She texted him. "He says he's back in the trees. He can see the abandoned railroad car from where he's at. The ghost town is beyond that."

Neil nodded. "I know how to find him. Text the others and tell them to park there as well. We will have to approach the area with caution and do it in some sort of two-by-two formation to see if we can figure out where they are before we make a move. What do you think?"

She nodded. "We need to use extreme caution." If Mitchell thought he was caught, there was no telling what he would do to the two people she loved most in the world.

"Like you said, maybe his intent was to lure us there." Neil turned the wheel so he veered off the road. The SUV rolled over some bushes. Agent Ferris's car came into view, tucked back in the trees and barely visible if she hadn't been looking for it.

Agent Ferris walked over to them before they had even gotten out of the car. "I did a little looking around the curve in the railroad tracks. There's a bunch of buildings. What is this place, anyway?"

"It was a railroad stop. The last resident moved out about 1960," Neil said.

Arielle gazed up the railroad tracks. "Did you see any sign that our suspect is here?"

Agent Ferris shook his head. "No sign of life anywhere."

"Let's split up and move in. Arielle will stay with me." He looked at Agent Ferris. "Text if you see anything. I can communicate with Charlie and Greg via radio." He pulled his phone out. "I'll let the other guys know that is the plan."

"I'll circle around the back if you two want to work your way along the railroad track." Agent Ferris pulled his gun and took off, dropping behind the first cluster of bushes that provided some cover.

"Stay close to me," Neil said to Arielle. "I can't begin to sort through this guy's motives. I only know that he has gone after you with intent to kill."

They hurried along the railroad tracks, using the overgrown brush as cover as much as they could. They ran past the train car that Ferris had mentioned. The tracks curved around and what used to be Telluride came into view. There were crumbling buildings on both sides of the tracks, along with a dilapidated train platform.

Neil leaned close to her and whispered, "One thing the estate auction owner told me was that they only had permission to go into the buildings that weren't deemed unsafe to enter."

"Which ones?" Arielle saw a lopsided building that might have held stores at one time and a three-story one that might have been a hotel.

"The theater and a couple of private residences," Neil said. His phone indicated he had a text. "The other two guys are here." He explained the plan and where they needed to be to provide backup. They were far enough away that his voice would not carry to the ghost town. Greg would go the same way Agent Ferris had gone, and Charlie would come up along the railroad tracks.

While Neil talked, she watched for any sign of movement. Her phone rang. Thinking it was from Agent Ferris, she looked down at her phone. Her throat went dry. It was from the number her mother had used—Mitchell Sandburg's burner phone. She pressed the connect button and put it on speaker so Neil could hear it as well.

"Time for you to die, Agent Olson. But first a little fun."

She shuddered as though hit by a blast of cold wind.

Neil leaned closer to her, shaking his head.

Mitchell hung up.

A second later her phone made a noise. She pressed the button that opened the text.

A picture of her mother tied up. Duct tape on her mouth.

She tilted the phone so Neil could see the photo. *Where was Zoe?*

She shook her head. "What does he even mean by that? Do you think he knows we found his hiding place? I'm going to call him."

"No." Neil grabbed her hand that held the phone. "Look at the photo. Those are old theater seats she's sitting in."

She looked again. The seat had been pulled from its row in the theater and was pushed against a wall with rose-patterned wallpaper.

"Let's surround the place and find your mom and Zoe. Get this guy once and for all."

Arielle nodded in agreement, but she could not let go of the concern that something bad had happened to her daughter. Was Mitchell saving that picture as the final torment?

Fending off rising panic, Neil radioed Greg and Charlie as to the plan.

Greg's voice came through the radio static. "Ferris and I are close together. I will let him know the plan. He can take the east side. I'll move to the north side of the theater. There's probably more than one entrance."

When Neil looked over his shoulder, Charlie was about twenty feet behind them. Each of them would take a side of the building and look for a way to gain entry. He radioed Charlie to take the west side of the building. "Arielle and I will go in the front."

Seeking out as much cover as they could, they moved toward the theater.

Did Mitchell know they were here, or had

he just sent his first threat thinking his hiding place had not been found out? Hopefully, they would be able to surprise him.

They drew closer to the two-story theater. The windows on the first floor were all broken. The marquee had fallen off and was leaning against the wall. Broken glass littered the area in front of the entrance.

Arielle gave him the hand signal that she was ready to move toward the south side of the theater. She unclicked the strap on her holster that held her gun in place and headed toward the overgrown brush on the side of the theater.

He moved in, drawing closer to the big double doors that now hung on their hinges. He gave a final glance to the second-story windows but didn't see any indication that anyone was up there.

Neil pulled his gun as he slipped into what once was the theater's lobby. The place was covered in dust. He checked the ticket booth and then moved through the wide doors to the main theater.

Arielle stayed close behind him as they stepped into the auditorium. More than three-quarters of the seats were missing or stacked against the wall. Stuffing from the chairs was strewn across the floor. The silence was disconcerting. Had he been wrong about where that photo was taken? Though it was hard to tell, it looked like Denise was in a small space—a powder room, perhaps, or a wide hallway.

Using hand signals, they split off, each of them moving down a separate aisle toward the orchestra pit. Ferris emerged from backstage with his weapon drawn. That meant Greg and Charlie had not gained entry.

Neil pointed up, indicating that they needed to search the balcony and projection area. Two staircases led to the second floor. Neil and Arielle took one while Ferris went up the other. Agent Ferris searched the balcony while Neil and Arielle headed toward the projection room at the back.

Neil noticed that the doorknobs to the projection room were missing. He waited until Arielle took up a position on the other side of the door with her gun pointed toward the ceiling. He kicked the door, and it swung open, creaking as it did so. If the suspect was in there, he only had one way out.

He stepped inside, gun drawn. Broken pieces of furniture and some metal film canisters littered the floor. The old clothes, bedding and empty soda cans and food containers strewn around indicated that someone may have squatted there in the past. There were no windows, but the room had a viewing window where the projector would have been looked out on the theater below.

"This isn't where they were kept. Mom would have been able to look through that opening and see the theater down below. That would have been the first thing she told me."

Neil tried to fathom what was going on.

Ferris stood in the doorway. "Nothing. I checked the restrooms as well."

Static came across Neil's radio. He pulled it from his belt and pressed the talk button.

"I think I found the car he used to get here. This one has been driven recently. All the others around here are busted up and rusty." Greg's voice came across the line. He paused between each statement as though he was walking around the car looking at it. "A dark sedan. Looks like the guy had a flat."

Through the radio, Neil could hear shots fired.

"Greg? Greg, are you okay?"

More shots.

NINETEEN

Arielle winced at the second volley of shots coming through the radio.

"Greg, are you there?" Neil's voice filled with anguish as they hurried down the stairs.

Agent Ferris was right behind them. They stepped out the front entrance to the theater, only to be greeted by more gunshots, this time aimed at them. The sound indicated that the bullets had come from a rifle, not a handgun. They all pressed against the outside wall of the theater.

The shots had come from the top of the railroad car. Why had they not thought to check the interior of the car? What if Mom and Zoe had been in there all along? The car could have had interior doors with the knobs missing. Theater chairs could have been moved there.

"We have to find Greg." Neil looked in one direction and then the other.

The vantage point from the top of the railroad car allowed Mitchell a 360 view. He must be lying flat so they couldn't see him. He could have climbed up there after they entered the theater, or he would have shot at them sooner. The car with the flat tire could be anywhere, and Greg might be lying beside it bleeding.

They could not move away from the front of building without being in the line of fire.

Agent Ferris crouched behind a stack of used two-by-fours and broken plywood and looked out toward the railroad car while Arielle and Neil slipped just inside the entrance so they still had a view of the railroad car through a window.

Neil pulled his radio off his belt. "Charlie, can you hear me?"

"I'm at the back of the building. I heard the shots but didn't see where they came from."

"Sandburg has taken up a position on the top of the railroad car. Do you have any idea which direction Greg went?"

"He never notified me of his position." Judging from how out of breath Charlie sounded, he must be moving while he talked.

"Did you see any sign of a drivable car back where you searched?"

"No. Nothing behind the theater. There

are cars there, but they clearly have not been driven for a long time. I'm working my way past the theater. I should have a view of the railroad car. Lots of cover out here, so I don't think he'll be able to see me."

"Roger that." Neil put his radio back on his belt.

"Maybe we should try and move in," said Agent Ferris. "He's outnumbered."

True, but Mitchell Sandburg also had a rifle and the high ground. The thing that worried Arielle the most, though, was that he would use her mom and Zoe as a way to escape. Were they tied up inside the railroad car? "I think we need to figure out where he has mom and Zoe and extricate them."

"We need to locate Greg, too." Neil shifted his weight. "Greg said it looked like the car had a flat, so Mitchell knows he has no means of escape."

"Based on everything I know about Mitchell Sandburg, he has some kind of plan worked up," Arielle said.

Agent Ferris indicated a pile of rubble not too far from the outside of the theater. "I'm going to try to get closer to that railroad car. If I swing in a wide arc and his attention is on you two, I might be able to get close enough to assess if the hostages are inside."

"Okay." Keeping her eyes on the top of the railroad car, Arielle moved out from the protection of the building. Neil was right behind her. Both of them moved along the exterior wall while Ferris crouched low and hurried toward the pile of rubble.

They came to the corner of the building and burst out. The first bit of brush would provide some cover. No shots were fired in their direction. Agent Ferris had made it even closer to the railroad car. She could barely see him crouching low in the brush. They moved again, and for a second or so, they were exposed. Still no shots.

Charlie's voice came across Neil's radio. "We have a problem." Again, it sounded like the older man was on the run and breathless.

"What is it?"

"Sandburg took one of the police cars. He's driving away. I saw him shove a woman in there."

Neil stood up. "Was there a little girl with him?"

"I don't know."

Arielle was already running back to where the cars had been parked. Neil fell in beside her. Within seconds, they overtook the older deputy. They all jumped into the same vehicle, with Neil behind the wheel.

They were close enough to the car that Mitchell had stolen to see the dust cloud he left behind on the dirt road. Arielle pulled out her phone and let Agent Ferris know what had happened and that they had left his vehicle behind.

Agent Ferris responded. "I found the car. It was on the other side of the railroad car." His voice dropped half an octave. "I found Greg."

"Is he okay?"

"I think he's been shot. Looks like the radio got shot up as well. He's conscious, but barely." Arielle heard mumbled noises, and then Ferris spoke again. "I gotta go. This man needs to get to a hospital."

Arielle drew her attention back to the road. "Agent Ferris found Greg. His injuries sounded serious. He's in good hands."

"Greg is more than a deputy. He's my friend."

The stolen vehicle was visible for just a moment on the straight stretch of road before it disappeared around a curve.

Arielle took in a deep breath as Neil accelerated. "Where do you think he's going?"

Neil addressed his comment to Charlie. "Any guesses?"

She did not know this area at all. Mitchell,

on the other hand, had lived here long enough to have explored back roads.

The older man leaned forward. "Depends on what his plan is. Clearly, he wants to get away, but we know he took the woman with him."

"And maybe my child." Arielle was so tense she could barely get the words out.

Please, God, she has to be okay. My baby has to be okay.

"His plan is to get away. He took the hostages because he thought he might need them." Neil stared at the road up ahead as he turned the wheel into a curve.

Once the road straightened out again, the other car came into view. They were still about the same distance from him.

Charlie said, "This road turns off in a few miles. He's probably not going to head back to town. Too much of a chance of being caught."

The countryside opened up as they passed rolling hills and fields planted with crops.

Neil veered off the road. "Let's hope you're right. I think I know how to cut him off." He drove through the fields. Mitchell's car had disappeared down the other side of a steep hill, which meant that Mitchell wouldn't see them cutting across the field.

Neil drove even faster. "We only have a

few seconds' lead time. When I stop, jump out and be ready for him."

"Because he has at least one hostage. We need to focus on disabling the vehicle," Arielle said.

Neil drove the car toward a cluster of trees by the road so it would not be as visible from far away. Mitchell wouldn't know he was about to be ambushed until it was too late.

All of them got out. Neil and Arielle took positions on one side of the road while Charlie moved to the other, shielded by some brush. Even before Arielle and Neil had lain down in the ditch, she heard Mitchell's car rolling toward them.

She pulled her weapon and lifted her head to get a visual. The car was moving at a high rate of speed, which meant he hadn't spotted their vehicle yet.

"I'll aim for the front tire." She waited until it felt like the car was almost on top of them.

Right before she took aim, Mitchell slowed. He'd spotted their car. Her breath caught. There was a chance he could just veer off the road and run them over.

She fired her shot when Mitchell's vehicle was only a few feet away. Neil and Charlie took aim just as the car rolled past, and then seemed to stutter and shake but kept going.

All of them jumped up and ran toward the car. Even before she closed the passenger-side door, Neil was racing back up to the road.

She only hoped they had disabled Mitchell's vehicle enough so he could not go far.

Neil rounded the curve.

Mitchell's car sat in the middle the road at an angle. Neil and Charlie got out with their guns drawn. She opened her car door and used it as a shield.

She heard a door slam. Mitchell came around the front end of the vehicle, which was halfway in the ditch. He held Denise in front of him. One hand must be securing her arm at a painful angle behind her, while the other held a knife to her mom's throat.

"Give me your car. Let me go and she can live."

Neil's heart pounded as he kept his weapon trained on Mitchell, who had positioned his body so Denise served as a shield. Taking a shot at this distance was too risky.

"Where's the child?" Neil adjusted his grip on the gun as sweat streamed past his temple.

Mitchell jerked Denise so she screamed. "We're only talking about one thing here. All of you need to move away from that car. I assume the keys are still in it."

Charlie inched closer to Mitchell off to the side, trying to line up a shot.

"One step closer and the lady gets it," Mitchell said.

Neil's breath caught when he saw a little blond head bob up above the windowsill and then disappear.

He looked into Mitchell's eyes. The man had killed many times before. He could kill Denise and still use Zoe as a bargaining chip.

Arielle stepped out from behind the car door. "You heard that man. Let's drop our weapons." She let her gun fall to the ground.

Arielle had weighed the odds and knew that she needed to save her mom, even if that meant Mitchell got away. He didn't know if Arielle had seen Zoe in the car.

Charlie dropped his weapon, and Neil followed.

Mitchell pushed Denise forward, still holding the knife to her throat. "All of you get over there across the road, hands in the air."

"When will you let my mother go?"

Mitchell didn't answer. Instead he edged toward the other car.

The three of them moved toward the opposite side of the road. Mitchell got closer to the driver's side of the functioning vehicle. Neil's view was partially obstructed, though he could see some of what was going on through the car windows.

Mitchell ordered Denise to start the car. He must still be holding the knife on her. A car door slammed. The car backed up. Denise lay on the ground. Arielle raced toward her. Charlie picked up a handgun as the car got farther away, still going in Reverse.

Neil ran toward the other car and flung the front driver's-side door open. Zoe was crouched down below the seat in the back. She looked up at Neil.

"You hold on, little girl. Stay there."

As he'd hoped, the rifle Mitchell had used was propped across the front passenger seat. He reached in, grabbed and aimed. While Arielle held her mother, Charlie made his way up the road. A handgun would not reach the car, but a rifle might. It was their only chance.

Neil looked through the scope and took aim at the front tire. He ratcheted another bullet into the chamber. This one went through the radiator. Mitchell kept backing up the car. There was no place to turn around. The car slipped into the bank as steam rolled out of the hood.

Neil took off running toward the SUV. He lifted the rifle when Mitchell got out, clearly preparing to run. Instead, he put his hands in the air. Charlie swooped in with his handgun drawn and pulled his handcuffs off his belt.

Neil turned and ran back to the car where Zoe was. He opened the back door. Zoe leaped into his arms. He held her, walking across the road to reunite mother and daughter.

TWENTY

Laughing and crying at the same time, Arielle reached out for her daughter. She held Zoe close, and Denise moved in to hug both of them.

"It's all right, baby." She stroked Zoe's hair as her heart swelled with joy.

Neil stood off to the side. "I'm just thankful she's okay." His eyes glazed.

Arielle looked directly at him. "So glad you were able to get to her."

In that moment, she realized that Neil loved Zoe as much as she did.

Charlie came over to them. He had handcuffed Mitchell and put him in the back of the car. "I already radioed for transport. I'll escort the prisoner. The city police will come in a separate car for the four of you."

"That would be good. I need to go by the hospital and check on Greg."

Arielle looked at Denise. "We'll go with you."

Denise nodded. "It is the least we can do."

While they waited for the car to show up, sadness washed over Arielle. Mitchell would be charged with kidnapping, enough to hold him until they could put together the case against him for the arson killings. He would be transported and held in a federal facility, where she could interview him. Her mom and Zoe would be able to head back to Denver before the day was over, and she would not be far behind after she wrapped up loose ends.

After that, she would never see Neil again. The thought grieved her deeply. They were two people from two very different worlds.

When the city police came to pick them up, Arielle sat in the back seat, holding Zoe close. Once they were at the hospital, she, Zoe and Denise sat in the waiting room while Neil went to check on his deputy.

Agent Ferris entered the waiting room.

Arielle rose to her feet and stepped away from her mom and Zoe. "How is Greg?"

"Bullet grazed him. When he fell, he hit his head. He'll be out of commission for a few days, but he'll be fine." Agent Ferris leaned closer to her. "I heard you got our man into custody."

"It was a team effort. I couldn't have done it without Neil, his deputy, and Agent Ferris."

"I'll put the paperwork through to transport him. We should be out of here in no time."

"Yes, in no time at all." Her heart ached at having to say that. She went to sit down by her mother. Zoe crawled into her lap. She held her close.

"I guess we'll be packing up and heading back home," Denise said.

"We'll need a statement from you, but it can wait." She stroked her daughter's hair. "You and Zoe have been through a lot."

"The whole trip wasn't awful. The farm was lovely, and I feel like Mary Ellen is a long-lost sister."

"It is nice here." Zoe had fallen asleep in her arms. "Slower pace of life. I will miss it." She realized in that moment what she would miss most was Neil.

Neil emerged from Greg's room at the end of the hallway.

Denise cupped her daughter's shoulder. "He looks like he wants to talk to you. I think I'll go see if I can find a hot cup of coffee."

Her mom stood up and walked in the opposite direction. Holding his cowboy hat, Neil made his way toward them.

"Looks like somebody conked out." His voice was filled with affection.

"She's been through a lot. I'm sure we'll have to see a counselor and have some talks." Arielle rested her hand on her daughter's head. "I don't ever want the people I love to be in the line of fire like that. I'm thinking about quitting the bureau."

He sat down beside her. "What would you do?"

"I'm not sure. It will take a while to figure out how to make that transition."

"You could be a part-time deputy in Wade County."

"Are you offering me a job?"

He turned to face her. "I'd like to offer you even more than that."

She was struck by the vastness of the emotion she saw in his eyes and the depth of sincerity in his expression. "Neil, I never thought I would feel affection for another man after losing Craig, but these last few days of being with you…"

"I never thought I could love again." He leaned in and kissed her. When he pulled back, he rested his hand on her cheek. His eyes searched hers. "I'd like you to be more than my part-time deputy. I'd like you to be my wife."

Joy flooded through her, and she saw clearly now what she had known all along. "I love you, Neil."

"I promise to be a good dad to Zoe."

"I know you will be."

"Arielle, will you marry me?"

"Yes, Neil, I will marry you."

He kissed her again.

Zoe stirred in her arms and opened her eyes, staring at Neil. "Hey, ladybug. Can I call you ladybug?"

Zoe nodded.

Neil gathered Arielle and Zoe into his arms.

Now both of them had the family they'd always longed for.

* * * * *

If you enjoyed this story, look for these other books by Sharon Dunn:

Undercover Mountain Pursuit
Alaskan Christmas Target

Dear Reader,

I hope you enjoyed the danger and excitement that Neil and Arielle faced together as they hunted down a killer. As I wrote this book, I thought about how a great deal of my childhood seemed to be sneaking into the story through the two older women in the book, Mary Ellen and Denise. I grew up in a small town that was like Silver Creek. Much of Montana is dotted with small towns and farms. I can remember going with my mom while she visited friends out in the country. The conversation always seemed to turn to the best way to pickle and can various garden products and how much sugar to put in the jams they made. I went chokecherry picking with my mom, and she grew rhubarb in her garden. Trust me, you have to put a lot of sugar in chokecherry and rhubarb jam to make it edible.

There is small moment in this story where Neil serves Arielle a homemade pickle that his mother made from a cucumber she grew. While the focus of this story needs to be on the romance and the suspense, I like that I could share something of the world I grew up in. In early drafts of the book, Neil's mom did not have a name. As the book unfolded, I realized I wanted to name her after my mother, Mary Ellen, as a tribute to her. How about you? What part of your childhood do you remember with fondness?

Sharon Dunn

Get 4 FREE REWARDS!
We'll send you 2 FREE Books plus 2 FREE Mystery Gifts.
FREE Value Over $20
Both the Love Inspired® and Love Inspired® Suspense series feature compelling novels filled with inspirational romance, faith, forgiveness, and hope.
YES! Please send me 2 FREE novels from the Love Inspired or Love Inspired Suspense series and my 2 FREE gifts (gifts are worth about $10 retail). After receiving them, if I don't wish to receive any more books, I can return the shipping statement marked "cancel." If I don't cancel, I will receive 6 brand-new Love Inspired Larger-Print books or Love Inspired Suspense Larger-Print books every month and be billed just $5.99 each in the U.S. or $6.24 each in Canada. That is a savings of at least 17% off the cover price. It's quite a bargain! Shipping and handling is just 50¢ per book in the U.S. and $1.25 per book in Canada.* I understand that accepting the 2 free books and gifts places me under no obligation to buy anything. I can always return a shipment and cancel at any time. The free books and gifts are mine to keep no matter what I decide.
Choose one: ☐ Love Inspired Larger-Print (122/322 IDN GNWC)
☐ Love Inspired Suspense Larger-Print (107/307 IDN GNWN)
Name (please print)
Address
Apt. #
City
State/Province
Zip/Postal Code
Email: Please check this box ☐ if you would like to receive newsletters and promotional emails from Harlequin Enterprises ULC and its affiliates. You can unsubscribe anytime.
Mail to the Harlequin Reader Service:
IN U.S.A.: P.O. Box 1341, Buffalo, NY 14240-8531
IN CANADA: P.O. Box 603, Fort Erie, Ontario L2A 5X3
Want to try 2 free books from another series? Call 1-800-873-8635 or visit www.ReaderService.com.
*Terms and prices subject to change without notice. Prices do not include sales taxes, which will be charged (if applicable) based on your state or country of residence. Canadian residents will be charged applicable taxes. Offer not valid in Quebec. This offer is limited to one order per household. Books received may not be as shown. Not valid for current subscribers to the Love Inspired or Love Inspired Suspense series. All orders subject to approval. Credit or debit balances in a customer's account(s) may be offset by any other outstanding balance owed by or to the customer. Please allow 4 to 6 weeks for delivery. Offer available while quantities last.
Your Privacy—Your information is being collected by Harlequin Enterprises ULC, operating as Harlequin Reader Service. For a complete summary of the information we collect, how we use this information and to whom it is disclosed, please visit our privacy notice located at corporate.harlequin.com/privacy-notice. From time to time we may also exchange your personal information with reputable third parties. If you wish to opt out of this sharing of your personal information, please visit readerservice.com/consumerschoice or call 1-800-873-8635. Notice to California Residents—Under California law, you have specific rights to control and access your data. For more information on these rights and how to exercise them, visit corporate.harlequin.com/california-privacy.
LIRLIS22

Get 4 FREE REWARDS!
We'll send you 2 FREE Books plus 2 FREE Mystery Gifts.
The Charming Checklist
HEATHERLY BELL
A Rancher's Touch
ALLISON LEIGH
FREE
Value Over
$20
The Wrong Cowboy
Sasha Summers
A Cowgirl's Secret
Melinda Curtis
Both the Harlequin® Special Edition and Harlequin® Heartwarming™ series feature compelling novels filled with stories of love and strength where the bonds of friendship, family and community unite.
YES! Please send me 2 FREE novels from the Harlequin Special Edition or Harlequin Heartwarming series and my 2 FREE gifts (gifts are worth about $10 retail). After receiving them, if I don't wish to receive any more books, I can return the shipping statement marked "cancel." If I don't cancel, I will receive 6 brand-new Harlequin Special Edition books every month and be billed just $4.99 each in the U.S or $5.74 each in Canada, a savings of at least 17% off the cover price or 4 brand-new Harlequin Heartwarming Larger-Print books every month and be billed just $5.74 each in the U.S. or $6.24 each in Canada, a savings of at least 21% off the cover price. It's quite a bargain! Shipping and handling is just 50¢ per book in the U.S. and $1.25 per book in Canada.* I understand that accepting the 2 free books and gifts places me under no obligation to buy anything. I can always return a shipment and cancel at any time. The free books and gifts are mine to keep no matter what I decide.
Choose one: ☐ Harlequin Special Edition (235/335 HDN GNMP) ☐ Harlequin Heartwarming Larger-Print (161/361 HDN GNPZ)
Name (please print)
Address
Apt. #
City
State/Province
Zip/Postal Code
Email: Please check this box ☐ if you would like to receive newsletters and promotional emails from Harlequin Enterprises ULC and its affiliates. You can unsubscribe anytime.
Mail to the Harlequin Reader Service:
IN U.S.A.: P.O. Box 1341, Buffalo, NY 14240-8531
IN CANADA: P.O. Box 603, Fort Erie, Ontario L2A 5X3
Want to try 2 free books from another series? Call 1-800-873-8635 or visit www.ReaderService.com.
*Terms and prices subject to change without notice. Prices do not include sales taxes, which will be charged (if applicable) based on your state or country of residence. Canadian residents will be charged applicable taxes. Offer not valid in Quebec. This offer is limited to one order per household. Books received may not be as shown. Not valid for current subscribers to the Harlequin Special Edition or Harlequin Heartwarming series. All orders subject to approval. Credit or debit balances in a customer's account(s) may be offset by any other outstanding balance owed by or to the customer. Please allow 4 to 6 weeks for delivery. Offer available while quantities last.

COUNTRY LEGACY COLLECTION
COUNTRY LEGACY
EMMETT
Diana Palmer
COUNTRY LEGACY
COURTED BY THE COWBOY
COUNTRY LEGACY
THE RANCHER AND THE BABY
Marie Ferrarella
19 FREE BOOKS IN ALL!
Cowboys, adventure and romance await you in this new collection! Enjoy superb reading all year long with books by bestselling authors like Diana Palmer, Sasha Summers and Marie Ferrarella!
YES! Please send me the Country Legacy Collection! This collection begins with 3 FREE books and 2 FREE gifts in the first shipment. Along with my 3 free books, I'll also get 3 more books from the Country Legacy Collection, which I may either return and owe nothing or keep for the low price of $24.60 U.S./$28.12 CDN each plus $2.99 U.S./$7.49 CDN for shipping and handling per shipment*. If I decide to continue, about once a month for 8 months, I will get 6 or 7 more books but will only pay for 4. That means 2 or 3 books in every shipment will be FREE! If I decide to keep the entire collection, I'll have paid for only 32 books because 19 are FREE! I understand that accepting the 3 free books and gifts places me under no obligation to buy anything. I can always return a shipment and cancel at any time. My free books and gifts are mine to keep no matter what I decide.
☐ 275 HCK 1939
☐ 475 HCK 1939
Name (please print)
Address
Apt. #
City
State/Province
Zip/Postal Code
Mail to the Harlequin Reader Service:
IN U.S.A.: P.O. Box 1341, Buffalo, NY 14240-8571
IN CANADA: P.O. Box 603, Fort Erie, Ontario L2A 5X3
*Terms and prices subject to change without notice. Prices do not include sales taxes, which will be charged (if applicable) based on your state or country of residence. Canadian residents will be charged applicable taxes. Offer not valid in Quebec. All orders subject to approval. Credit or debit balances in a customer's account(s) may be offset by any other outstanding balance owed by or to the customer. Please allow 3 to 4 weeks for delivery. Offer available while quantities last. © 2021 Harlequin Enterprises ULC. ® and ™ are trademarks owned by Harlequin Enterprises ULC.
Your Privacy—Your information is being collected by Harlequin Enterprises ULC, operating as Harlequin Reader Service. To see how we collect and use this information visit https://corporate.harlequin.com/privacy-notice. From time to time we may also exchange your personal information with reputable third parties. If you wish to opt out of this sharing of your personal information, please visit www.readerservice.com/consumerschoice or call 1-800-873-8635. Notice to California Residents—Under California law, you have specific rights to control and access your data. For more information visit https://corporate.harlequin.com/california-privacy.
50BOOKCL22